W. M. Tarrant grew up in rural West Central Illinois with a wide-open view of the sky. He watched airliners, some of them propeller-driven, fly high overhead, leaving their telltale contrails, while Cessna and Piper airplanes flew about down low. In the Military Operations Area airspace, fighter planes practiced maneuvers, streaking by at near supersonic speeds. This aerial activity, along with books about seaplanes and flying boats, sparked a life-long interest in aviation and led to this book.

He and his wife reside in Galesburg, Illinois, home of the annual National Stearman Fly-In. He is a member of the American Aviation Historical Society.

Engines Over the Amazon

A Novel of Seaplanes in the 1930s

AIA PUBLISHING

W.M.TARRANT

Engines Over the Amazon

Copyright © 2021

Published by AIA Publishing, Australia

ABN: 32736122056

http://www.aiapublishing.com

All characters in this publication are fictitious and any resemblance to real persons, living or dead, is purely coincidental.

All rights reserved. No part of this publication may be reproduced, stored in a retrieval system or transmitted in any form or by any means electronic, mechanical, audio, visual or otherwise, without prior permission of the copyright owner. Nor can it be circulated in any form of binding or cover other than that in which it is published and without similar conditions including this condition being imposed on the subsequent purchaser.

ISBN: 978-1-922329-21-9

Cover design by Rose Newland

Acknowledgements

Thank you to my parents for instilling the value of education.

A big thank you to my wife for her support and encouragement.

My editor Tahlia Newland and her staff at AIA publishing helped tremendously by correcting and polishing my writing.

Thanks to Katherine Kirk of Gecko Edit, who did the proofreading.

Introduction

Part of the inspiration for this story are the early days of Pan American Airlines as it ventured into South America. By 1934 the airline was well established in the Caribbean and South America. The author took creative license with the timeline for a couple of reasons. He wanted to feature the Sikorsky S-42 which first flew in 1934. Also the growing tensions in the world form an integral part of the story, specifically the threat from the Nazi Party in Germany which gained power in 1933 when Adolf Hitler became chancellor.

The general historical background is accurate to the best of the author's knowledge.

Understand that this is not a flight manual for the S-42 nor for any other airplane. The crew positions depicted in the story are correct, though some of the instruments and controls described come from the author's imagination.

A short-lived airline named Caribbean Airways operated in the Caribbean from 1930 to 1932. Today, there is a Caribbean Airlines headquartered in Port of Spain, Trinidad and Tobago. The fictitious airline in this story is not to be confused with either of these air carriers or with any other airline.

Flying Boats

During the age of the flying boat, expansive, multiengine airplanes with boat-like fuselages carried people in luxury across vast expanses of water. After a powerful takeoff, the sleek boat of the air soared gracefully through the sky toward a faraway destination, the tropical sun glimmering brightly off the shiny aluminum. The hungry, three-bladed propellers bit off great bites of air and pulled the plane through the sky, seemingly effortless. At the destination, the machine touched down on water, creating a wake that rose feet into the air then gradually faded as the plane slowed and eased to a stop at a dock.

These graceful yet powerful yachts of the air symbolized the elegance and privilege that existed for a select few through the darkness of the Great Depression. Passengers dressed in finery—women with elegant long dresses, slouch hats, and jewelry, and men in tailored pin-striped suits and fedoras set rakishly on pomaded hair—rode the planes to exotic ports of call. These passengers looked down on the world below, literally and figuratively, aloof from the desperation of the masses. As they winged their way through the skies, they dined on fine food served on elegant china as the desperate of the world below scrounged for a morsel of bread or a cup of soup.

Chapter One

Caribbean Airways pilot Jack Smith listened intently as John Trapp spoke. Jack, along with Captain Max Williams and mechanic Ed Butz, stood in Trapp's office. The Spartan room contained a large wooden desk and pictures on the walls of Caribbean Airways planes—the Consolidated Commodore and the line of Sikorsky models, the S-36, S-38, and S-40.

Trapp, dressed in a dark blue pin-striped suit, red necktie, and glossy black wingtip shoes, was tall, broad shouldered, and square jawed. An imposing man of courage and vision, he left the comfortable life and guaranteed wealth of his family in order to pursue his dream of owning an airline. His airline would not be just one of the many regional carriers sprouting up over the country but would become an international giant carrying people, goods, and mail to the farthest corners of the globe. That was his vision.

He stood beside a large world globe mounted in an ornate wooden frame and spun it slowly as he talked. Trapp, known as the old man by Caribbean Airways employees, stopped the globe and tapped on it to emphasize a point. Then he walked over to a wall map and, pointing, said, "Gentlemen, take a look at this map. These blue lines represent our current routes; those in red represent future routes. As you can see, we want to go even deeper into South America."

The blue line stopped at Georgetown, British Guiana. He pointed to the red line that went from Georgetown down along the east coast of South America all the way to Buenos Aires. "The new plane from Sikorsky, their S-42 model, will help make it feasible. It's fifty miles per hour faster than our Commodores and S-40s and can carry more passengers and payload. And now we have the mail contract for the entire route to guarantee income. But I do want to see the passenger business increase. I want the planes full of freight and passengers to give us money over and above the mail contract."

Trapp had built his airline through hard work and shrewd business dealings, some of those dealings not sitting well with competitors, especially Randolph McClelland, founder of the former Eastern South American Airways. It was rumored he still held a grudge and would stop at nothing to put Caribbean Airways out of business. McClelland, a fighter ace of the Great War, was known for his daring and aggressiveness in the air and on the ground. He'd lost out on a mail contract to South America to Trapp and his airline after Trapp used his political influence and inside dealings with the United States Post Office to get his way. Forced to sell, McClelland sold his airline for pennies on the dollar. McClelland's last words to Trapp were, "Someday, you're gonna pay!"

"I'm depending on you three men to evaluate this new plane," Trapp said. "Be honest. Anything that needs improving, Sikorsky will do. They want to sell planes; we need planes that will do the job."

"Yes sir," said Captain Williams. "We'll put the plane through the wringer. We have the best mechanic anywhere right here in Ed Butz. He'll find anything that's not right."

Captain Williams was chief pilot for Caribbean Airways. A tall, slender man with dark hair parted on the left side, held in place with pomade, and a thin, neatly trimmed mustache, he presented the image of the dapper, confident pilot. The uniform fit him perfectly: dark blue pants and jacket with four gold stripes on the cuffs and a white shirt and dark blue necktie. A white sea captain-style cap with the Caribbean Airways logo emblazoned on the front—a pair of gold wings protruding from a world globe—topped off the uniform.

Ed Butz, head of maintenance, had been a fighter pilot in the Great War, ending the war in a German prison camp after going down behind enemy lines. A short, stout man with a head of messy brown hair and a thick, drooping mustache, he wore blue coveralls with the airline logo embroidered on the back.

The first officer, Jack Smith, was a Missouri farm boy, tall and slim, but without the dash of Captain Williams. His uniform lacked the crispness of the captain's, and he perpetually fought with a shirttail that refused to remain tucked. A trace of Midwest twang still lingered in his speech though he hadn't lived in Missouri for over eight years.

"I'm counting on him and you two pilots," Trapp said.

"Sir, do we have a radio operator?" Jack asked. "I understand this new plane has a station for a radio man."

"Yes, I've hired a fellow from RCA. He also served in the Army Signal Corps and worked with radios there. Smart fella who's made some innovations to radio communication and radio navigation. He's come up with a new transmitter that increases effective distance. Somehow the radio signal can go beyond the horizon. He can explain it to you. This fellow, Harold Newman, will meet you in Stratford.

"I anticipate expansion, some of it quite rapid," Trapp continued. "We're changing the world, you and I and all of Caribbean Airways. Hell, the other airlines are too. Our entire industry is changing the world, making it smaller. The airplane is effectively shrinking the globe. And Caribbean Airways is going to lead the way, damn it, so we have to expand and do so as quickly as possible. It's almost the middle of 1934, and the depression isn't showing signs of ending anytime soon, but hell, there's always people with money. Air travel is faster than boats, and we'll make it even more luxurious than the ships—fine food, waiters, ornate interiors on the planes. This new plane from Sikorsky will be even nicer than our S-38s, and it's faster and can carry thirty-two passengers. I want all seats filled. I know it won't happen right off, but with the right promotion it will happen.

"I want you fellas to survey the route down to Buenos Aires. Check out the facilities at the various communities, docks, terminals, fuel supplies. Make sure the routes are feasible and that we have what we need at each destination."

"Yes sir," said Captain Williams.

"Be ready to go as soon as you get the plane to Nassau and ready for flight. We'll add a temporary navigator's station in the passenger cabin for these initial flights. Once it's completed, I want you on your way."

"Yes sir."

"You need to be alert because there may be competition from Colombia and South American Airways," Trapp continued. "In fact, they may be a downright threat. The new German government has been working with them, supplying airplanes and equipment. I also understand there are some German pilots flying for them now. There's concern they may try to get into Panama. We can't let that happen because of the canal."

"I've heard the same thing," Jack said. "There's bad things going on in Germany. That new chancellor, Hitler, that got elected last year, seems to have some wild ideas. That Nazi party of his sounds pretty crazy. It's only a matter of time until he has total control of Germany."

Trapp nodded. "That's what my connections in Washington say. They feel Germany is trying to get a firm foothold here in the Western Hemisphere. If they do and they get control of the canal, well, you can just imagine what that will mean."

"What about McClelland?" Jack asked.

"Him! That sore loser! I think he's moved on. I wouldn't worry about him."

Trapp shook hands with each man and said, "Good luck, men. Oh, and I want daily reports. Now get going and get to Stratford."

The men had traveled to New York City and the airline's corporate headquarters the day before from Caribbean Airways operations headquarters in Nassau, Bahamas. Now they took a cab back to the hotel, The New Yorker, where they'd stayed the previous night. They sat comfortably in the roomy cab—a Checker Model K, yellow with black fenders and running boards as well as the trademark black and white checkered stripe along each side. The driver, a gum-chomping middle-aged man with his fedora hat tilted rakishly, sat apart from the passengers. This separation of driver and passengers as well as the long 127-inch wheelbase of the cab created a limousine-like experience. The six-cylinder Buda engine purred quietly.

Horns honked. People crowded the sidewalks, men in suits and those dressed more casually—open collar and no tie—and women in long skirts that fluttered and swirled in the breeze, head scarves keeping hair in place. People and cars and horse-drawn wagons filled the streets and sidewalks in the valleys between the tall buildings. The

Chrysler Building and the even taller Empire State Building dominated the skyline. Street vendors and newsboys hawked their wares at the mass of people hurrying past.

The cab shared the road with V-16-powered Cadillacs whose long hoods matched the long noses of their owners—Auburns, Chevrolets, Chryslers, and Fords, lots of Fords, both the Model T and the newer Model A, being the most prolific cars on the streets. The Model Ts all were black because Henry Ford said a person could order them in any color as long as it was black.

The taxi passed a line of people on a dingy sidewalk waiting for free food, one of the many bread lines of the era. The people in the ragged line—the hardest hit victims of the Great Depression—hung their heads, and when they did look up, intense desperation and sadness lined their faces.

Only a few blocks later, they arrived at The New Yorker, a hotel symbolic of luxury with an art deco lobby and rooms ranging in price from $3.50 up. The men each had their own room, and though the cheapest in the hotel, they were still first-rate, each with a radio, a tub, and a shower.

The night before, they'd visited the hotel's famed Terrace Room and enjoyed the music of the Casa Loma Orchestra—one of the first big bands—which played songs including "The Casa Loma Stomp," "No Name Jive," and "Maniac's Ball," as well as their signature tune, "Smoke Rings." The band performed on a stage at one end of the room, and chairs and tables, set along walls lined with ornate curtains, surrounded the dance floor in the middle. While the captain and Jack listened to the music and watched the dancers, Ed, to their astonishment, spent the evening cutting a rug with every available female dancer.

Now, after hastily shedding their Caribbean Airways uniforms and donning suits and narrow ties, they packed their bags and left. They walked through the tunnel that connected The New Yorker to the train station to begin their trip to the Sikorsky Aircraft Factory in Stratford, Connecticut. Jack and Captain Williams sported hats, but Ed remained bareheaded, his bushy hair in disarray and his perpetual cigar clamped between his teeth, though out of respect for the two nonsmoking pilots, he left it unlit in the confines of the train car.

The New York Central Railroad coal-burning steam engine chugged across the countryside, a steady column of black smoke pouring from the stack and swirling in a long cloud back across the length of the train. In Stratford they planned to spend a couple of days learning the new aircraft's systems and doing air work under the guidance of a Sikorsky test pilot, aiming to perfect their skills with the new machine before flying it to Nassau.

Captain Williams pulled a manila envelope from his flight bag and said, "The old man gave me this just before we left. It's the specifications and procedures for the new plane. Let's use this time to go over them, so we'll have a little bit of familiarity by the time we get to the factory."

"You two go ahead," Ed said. "I've got all the stuff memorized."

"How?" Jack asked. "We just got this information."

"You just got it. I ran across a copy a couple of weeks ago."

"But how?"

Ed didn't reply.

During the war, Ed Butz flew the Sopwith Camel, an effective, highly maneuverable pursuit plane, but one that was also highly treacherous, killing more pilots through accidents than were killed in enemy action. Ed had a knack with machines and flew the tricky plane flawlessly, and he also worked with the mechanics to keep it in top condition. But he was most remembered by his ability to mysteriously procure items that no one else could find: fresh vegetables, fresh meat, chocolate, alcohol, cigarettes, engine parts—all rare items in war-torn northwestern

France in summer 1918. He never divulged his secrets or allowed anyone to accompany him, but everyone appreciated what he could acquire, so they never pressed him very hard. His reputation continued sixteen years later.

Jack and Captain Williams were too young to have served in the war, but they joined the military as soon as they turned eighteen, Jack in 1924 and the captain in 1922. Jack served in the Army Air Corps and Captain Williams flew with the navy.

Next morning, a Sikorsky company car took the men to the factory to meet the new airplane and the chief test pilot. The Sikorsky factory sprawled across 124 acres that abutted the shore of the Housatonic River near its mouth where it flowed into Long Island Sound. Forty-nine buildings comprised the plant, built in 1929. Smaller buildings and massive, long buildings made up the complex. An eight-hundred-foot-long earthen causeway extended into the river to provide access for the seaplanes the factory produced. A handful of planes rocked gently at their docks.

Chief test pilot Leonard Morris met the men at the gate. A tall, slender man, clean-shaven, soft-spoken and with an easy smile, he held himself with a quiet confidence, without the usual test pilot swagger. He wore a white shirt and black tie, but no suitcoat, and his shiny black wingtip shoes glistened in the sunlight. He took them to one of the long buildings, an expansive, high-ceilinged structure, where dozens of airplanes rested in various stages of assembly. Workers crawled over them like ants as they secured, riveted, and fastened parts. The men followed him into a windowless office containing a long table covered in charts, graphs, and pages of instructions pertaining to the new airplane. On a chalkboard mounted on one wall, someone had drawn diagrams, numbers, and math formulas in white chalk.

"Today we'll spend our time going through the operating manual, learning the systems and procedures," Leonard explained. "I've got updated manuals for you that include handwritten notes from myself and the other test pilots. Eventually the changes will be incorporated into the printed manual, but for now, use the references penciled in. Actually, between you and me, I'd like to hold the plane for some more testing, but Trapp wrangled it a tad early."

"Do you have any particular concerns?" the captain asked.

"Nothing in particular. Everything seems to be working fine, but I'd just like to check it out a little more, I suppose, for my own peace of mind."

"When do we get to fly?" Jack asked.

"Tomorrow. But we'll go to the dock to see the plane this afternoon and go through familiarization."

After a morning of detailed instruction on the systems, procedures, operation, and nuances of the airplane, the men ate lunch in the factory cafeteria, where they met the radio operator for the upcoming flight.

"This is Harold Newman," Leonard indicated the gray-suited man sitting at the table. "He used to work for RCA, and he knows his radios. He's refined the navigation radio, the direction-finding radio that homes in on a station. He's also modified transmitters for radio waves to go beyond the horizon. You can see the usefulness of that out over the ocean. He can explain it all to you sometime. He's also improved the voice communication radios, making it easier to change frequencies. No more changing coils, just turning knobs."

Harold didn't look up, just continued to eat. He wore his reddish-brown wavy hair combed straight back, and had horn-rimmed glasses with thick lenses.

"Glad to have you on the crew, Mister Newman," the captain said.

Without looking up, Harold said, "It's not Mister Newman, it's Harold."

Jack cringed. No one talked to Captain Williams in this manner.

Ed smiled.

"I spent time in the military," Harold said. "All I

heard was Corporal Newman this, Corporal Newman that. I'm tired of that formal stuff."

The captain nodded. "Well, Harold, glad to have you on the crew. I understand you worked with radios in the military."

"That's right. Army Signal Corps." Harold finally looked up from his plate. "After four years there, I went to work at RCA."

"How'd you end up here?" the captain asked.

"John Trapp offered me more money than RCA. Also, I'm to be in charge of radio communication and repair."

"Have you been up in the new plane?" asked Jack.

"Twice."

"What's it like?"

"I don't care for it."

"Why not?"

"I don't like to fly."

"What?" Jack frowned. "Then why did you take this job?"

"I'd never flown before, but figured there'd be nothing to it. I was wrong."

"You never flew in the army?" Jack asked.

"I said I was in the Signal Corps, not the Flying Corps." Harold turned away and focused on his food.

Ed was about to burst out laughing. Jack and Captain Williams sat in silence.

"We have air-to-ground voice communication in our planes," the captain said. "We're the first airline to do so."

Harold nodded. "I've heard; but we'll need to update the radios. The new ones are more efficient, offer clearer communication, easier to use in the long run, but it'll take some training to learn them. And then there's the navigation radio on the new planes, so you're going to need a dedicated radio operator. There's too much for just a pilot to do. I'm going to train radio men—part of my job is being in charge of communications for the airline."

"That's what I understand," the captain said. "The new planes have a station for a radio operator. I imagine that will be standard on all planes in the future, at least the ones designed for long distance."

Leonard said, "I've seen the drawings for the next couple of projects, and the four-engine planes are four-crew machines: two pilots, radio, and flight mechanic. I hear Martin's working on a four-engine flying boat. Same basic layout, four-man crew. Maybe even a navigator station."

"If they're thinking of going across the ocean, they're going to need a navigator," the captain said.

"I think the old man is looking at the Atlantic, then the Pacific," Ed said.

Jack nodded. "We're going to need something

with even more range than the S-42."

"It's coming," Leonard said. "In a few years, there'll be planes flying all over the globe. The technology is coming."

Having finished his meal, Harold pulled out a pipe and a tin of tobacco and began filling and packing the pipe. He worked slowly and deliberately to get it just right, then lit it with a silver Zippo and puffed on it to get it to draw. The smoke curled up around his head as it drifted toward the ceiling.

Ed clamped down on a fresh cigar. "Smells pretty good, Harold, though I'm a cigar man myself. That some kind of special tobacco?"

"Just Prince Albert Cherry Vanilla. You can get it anywhere."

After lunch, the men went to the dock. The sleek new airplane sat there, glistening in the brilliant sunshine, the biggest airplane the Caribbean Airways men had ever seen. The twin vertical tails towered seventeen feet in the air, and portholes lined the sixty-nine-foot-long boat-shaped fuselage. The wing sat above the fuselage on a streamlined pylon stretching 114 feet wingtip to wingtip. Four Pratt & Whitney Hornet nine-cylinder 750-horsepower radial engines rested in streamlined nacelles that blended into the leading edge of the wing. Though the plane weighed thirty thousand more pounds than the S-38, thanks to streamlining and variable-pitch propellers and other engineering feats, it cruised fifty miles per hour faster.

Jack grinned. "Wow! Some airplane!"

"It is impressive, isn't it?" Leonard smiled. "Wait till we get inside where it's even more impressive."

After examining the outside of the aircraft, with Leonard explaining the machine's features, the men entered the plane through the door at the rear of the flight deck. Inside, the men sat at their stations and, with direction from Leonard, became familiar with the controls, with all their buttons, switches and knobs. Two sets, one per pilot, of four throttles and four propeller controls hung down from an overhead console. Gauges, instruments, and more knobs and switches, as well as the massive control wheel and rudder pedals sat in front of each pilot. A trim wheel for each pilot was mounted beside the pilots' seats and could be rotated to adjust the trim of the elevators.

Ed Butz settled into his station, his seat ninety degrees to the pilots' seats, facing the center of the flight deck. In addition to the gauges, valves, and maze of wires and pipes, the flight mechanic's station had a full set of engine controls.

Taking it all in, Ed smiled. This was his element where he would control fuel flow and fuel mixtures and monitor and control engine functions.

Harold, already familiar with the radios, sat quietly, seemingly bored, puffing on his pipe, as the other men touched, studied, and felt controls and, in their minds, already had the great machine airborne. Leonard explained the functions of the array of switches, knobs, and gauges and went over procedures and emergency operations.

Around sunset, the men concluded their session, and the three men from Nassau returned to the hotel where they studied the revised manuals with the notes, comments, figures, and charts penciled in by the test pilots. Just outside the hotel, a man in a threadbare suit held a worn, wrinkled, and stained carboard sign with the words "out of work, can you spare a dime?" scrawled in black ink. All three airmen emptied their pockets of change and gave it to the man, who thanked them profusely. The men said nothing to each other because there wasn't much to say.

Jack opened the aircraft manual. "There's a lot of new stuff to remember; it's going to take me all night to learn even half of it."

Ed nodded. "They've added so much new information, it's gonna take me awhile to catch on and unlearn some of the stuff I thought I knew. They need to get a revised manual printed real soon. This isn't gonna work with all these handwritten notes in the margins."

Rather than take the time to go eat, the men ordered room service. They studied and memorized critical information until their eyes glazed over. Then they collapsed into their beds.

Next morning at the dock, under Leonard's guidance, all four men went through the exterior preflight steps, then climbed aboard. Ground crewmen stood by to untie the securing ropes.

The flight crew settled into their respective seats. Captain Williams offered the command pilot's seat on the left to Jack, giving him the honor of first flight. Leonard took the copilot's seat, where he would direct Jack through the various maneuvers, and Captain Williams knelt just behind them in order to observe. Leonard guided the men through the engine starting sequence, and one by one the four big engines came to life. The giant machine rocked in time to the idling engines and the big three-blade propellers as they turned over lazily, easily. When all was ready, the ground crew untied the ropes. Jack eased the throttles forward, and the big plane pulled slowly away from the dock. On the way to the takeoff and landing lane, Jack made the engine checks, and when they reached the lane, he lined up the plane, pulled the throttles to idle, and took a deep breath. He felt anticipation and excitement at learning a new aircraft, and also, though an experienced aviator, nervous at the controls—a common feeling among pilots, no matter how great their experience.

Jack felt just as he had years ago, the first time he sat at the controls of the twin-engine Keystone Bomber, a plane much bigger than the single-engine training aircraft he'd flown previously.

"It flies just like an airplane," his instructor had said. "It's just bigger but has all the same controls."

Jack had soon mastered the big machine, guiding it smoothly and confidently through the skies. He tried to remember that now as his hands sweated, his mouth dried, and butterflies fluttered in his stomach. Then he reached overhead for the throttles and pushed them forward.

"Easy!" Ed said. "Don't over boost the engines."

Jack paused a moment, then resumed advancing the throttles, this time slowly and smoothly. The big plane accelerated slowly, then at an increasing rate. Water sprayed up and back, splashing over the bow and past the pilots' windows. The nose rose slightly, then pointed higher as speed increased. Jack felt the plane getting lighter on the water, felt it dancing around, just skimming the surface. Then it lifted into the air. He realized he'd been holding his breath, and now, the plane free of the water, he began to breathe again.

Ed adjusted the fuel mixtures for the engines and watched the gauges, monitoring engine speed, manifold and oil pressure, oil and cylinder temperature, and fuel quantity and pressure indicators. Eyes in constant motion, he scanned the four sets of gauges, twenty in all, making sure each reading remained within the safe zone.

When they reached a thousand feet of altitude, Leonard directed Jack to make propeller and engine adjustments. He reduced engine power slightly and increased the pitch of the propellers so they'd take a bigger bite of air. At cruise, the blade angle would be increased even more, so the propellers could turn slower, requiring less engine power.

They leveled off at four thousand feet. Jack made a final adjustment to the propeller pitch and engine power and trimmed the plane for level flight. Leonard then took Jack through flight maneuvers— steep turns, stalls, and slow flight—to help him learn the characteristics of the airplane throughout various phases of flight and so become intimately acquainted with the machine.

He banked the plane into a forty-five-degree angle to perform a steep turn, the increase in G-force pushing the men down in their seats. The nose dropped. Jack pulled back on the control wheel, the nose rose, and the G-force pressed harder on the men. Captain Williams, though kneeling on the floor, remained calm, but Harold grabbed the edge of his table.

"Roll out," Leonard instructed calmly.

Jack leveled the wings.

"You lost a couple of hundred feet there," Leonard said. "Notice how quickly it happened? Try it again, but add a little power this time to help keep the nose up. You'll find that useful on this plane."

Again, Jack banked the plane over to forty-five degrees, adding a bit of engine power and, as Leonard said, the plane easily maintained altitude. Jack completed a full circle to the left, rolled the wings level, then promptly went into a steep turn to the right.

Next, Leonard had Jack configure the plane for slow flight, reducing power yet holding altitude. He gradually reduced the airspeed, and when they reached flap extension speed, he lowered the flaps incrementally until they were fully extended. In order to maintain altitude, he opened the throttles to full power, keeping the airspeed just above the minimum to maintain flight. To headings requested by Leonard, he made gentle, shallow bank turns, nudging the big plane around. If he was too aggressive on the controls, the plane would stall, quit flying, and go into an earthward descent. Flying the plane in this manner revealed its characteristics and the true ability of the pilot. Both were on the edge of control. Slow flight gave the pilot a feel for the plane at the speed with which landings were made, when they slowed just feet above the landing surface as the wings gave up lift and the plane settled onto the water. The controls felt different, reacted differently, slower to respond, requiring more movement compared to cruise flight. In cruise, the plane nearly flew itself, but in this slow regime, the pilot had to be precise, exact, fully in command. Jack smiled to himself as he felt the plane respond to his inputs, this big machine at his command.

"Resume normal flight," Leonard said.

Jack lowered the nose slightly to gain airspeed, and as speed increased, he raised the flaps—those hinged sections on the wing's trailing edge that could be lowered to produce more lift and increase drag, thus allowing the plane to fly slower. The flaps went from just inside the ailerons across the full length of the wing's center section, and when fully hung out they allowed a steep descent at a low airspeed. Without the aid of flaps, the S-42 would have a landing speed too high to be safe; the flaps allowed it to land at sixty-five miles per hour. Once the plane was reconfigured for cruise flight, Leonard gave instructions to set up for a stall.

At the mention of the word "stall," Harold braced himself and looked straight ahead at his radios.

With throttles back to idle and nose gradually brought up to hold altitude, the angle of the plane increased. In order to continue producing the lift required to remain flying, the wings struck the air at a higher angle, but finally the angle became too high, and the airflow over the wings separated. Lift destroyed, the plane dropped, gravity pulling it earthward. The left wing dropped slightly. Jack leveled it. The nose still pointed upward, but the plane fell downward, the altimeter unwinding as the water below came up to meet them.

"Better recover," Leonard said calmly.

Jack released back pressure on the control wheel and added full engine power, but the plane still descended, now nose-down. The altimeter kept unwinding, ticking off the decreasing distance to the water below. The engines revved up, and the propellers clawed the air as the surface of the ocean grew closer by the second. With airspeed still below stall, the needle crept upward, and finally the wings produced enough lift to hold up the plane. Jack eased gently back on the yoke, and the altimeter stabilized, then gradually showed an altitude increase.

"Lost quite a bit of altitude, didn't we?" Leonard said.

"I'll say. Do this close to the ground and we'd run out of sky."

"Exactly the point."

After a few minutes of straight, level flight, they turned back to the landing area at Stratford to practice takeoffs and landings. Upon touching down, Jack reconfigured the plane, added power, and took off, then circled back and landed again. Half a dozen times, he repeated this procedure in order to learn the intricacies of landing—making a proper approach, setting the propellers correctly, and using the correct power settings. After that Captains Williams took a turn in the pilot seat—his chance to go through the maneuvers and gain a feel for the aircraft.

Ed diligently monitored engines and systems operation throughout the flight, becoming familiar with the location of each gauge, switch, and lever. He settled into a routine and gained confidence in his position. Harold was little more than a passenger—a timid one—though he did turn on the radios and run checks on them. Both nonpilots benefited from experiencing the plane in its different phases of flight. They'd now know what to expect and feel, and they'd know what was normal and what wasn't—knowledge and experience that could prove valuable in the future.

The sun hung low in the sky when the men taxied

the plane into its docking berth and secured it for the night. It would wait patiently for their return and the flight to its new home in Nassau.

Stock Crash

The Roaring Twenties screeched to a halt on Monday, October 28, 1929, when the stock market crashed, beginning a slide that lasted until November 1932—and even then recovery was years away. It affected all but the most remote places in the world. Practically overnight, the country went from the Jazz Age to the Sad Age. People lost money, banks closed, businesses went under, and destitution swept the nation and the world. People stood in breadlines, their faces worry-worn, their posture that of discouragement as they shuffled along, desperate for anything to give their life meaning again.

The styles and life of the 1920s—women with bobbed hair and straight, shapeless dresses and headbands and men in pin-striped suits enjoying the good life of prosperity and frivolity—became a distant memory. Speakeasies opening their doors to passwords and coded knocks, the Charleston, the fox-trot, and jazz combos lost all meaning as the world slogged through the depths of the Great Depression. Prohibition remained in effect until December 5, 1933, when people once again could sit on stools along well-worn bars and openly drown their sorrows and bury their grief.

The desperate economy reached all corners of the country, from the dirty sidewalks and skyscrapers to the remote farm communities. Belts tightened everywhere. Nothing was wasted. Clothes were patched, and patched some more, until just threads were left. Only a select few escaped the desperation.

Chapter Two

The next morning, gray clouds, long and low, hugged the earth, and a strong wind whipped around the buildings, scattering debris down the dingy streets. The people on the bustling sidewalks wore coats buttoned up to the neck, collars turned up. The men held their fedoras tightly to their heads, and the women wore securely tied scarves. Everyone walking into the wind leaned forward slightly; those walking with the wind were pushed along.

When the men arrived at the Sikorsky factory, they checked the updated weather report. It indicated a strong storm with wind, rain, and snow barreling toward the northeast. And it was cold, the air temperature in the low thirties with a biting, stinging windchill. The cold especially affected the three men who were used to tropical air. Despite wearing gloves and being bundled up with two shirts under their jackets, they shuddered and shook, the cold penetrating to their bones.

Harold and Leonard, dressed warmly in thick gloves and heavy coats, collars turned up, seemed immune to the cold. Harold smirked at the three freezing men who'd forgotten the bitter, windswept landscape that could be vicious even in April.

"Sure you want to head out today?" Leonard asked. The men were back outdoors after the temporary warmth of Leonard's office. "A storm's approaching from the southwest. Coming pretty quickly too."

"Looks like there's going to be a stretch of bad weather," Captain Williams said. "This may be the best shot for several days. If we get south of the storm before it intensifies, we should be good the rest of the way home."

"Suit yourself. But you fellas are welcome to stay here as long as you like. We'll put you up for the duration."

"We may have to take you up on that. We'll see what happens in the next forty-five minutes or so while we prepare for flight."

Leonard nodded. "All right, suit yourself. I'll help you with preflight, make sure all's in order."

The plane, which had gleamed in the bright

sunlight the day before, now loomed ominously over the dock, no longer bright, but gray as the early morning sky. The waves slapped the side of the hull, and the plane rocked, not gently or soothingly now, but with force that tugged at the securing ropes. They creaked under the strain.

The men climbed aboard, secured their suitcases in the luggage compartment, then went to their crew stations and stowed flight gear and Thermos bottles of hot coffee. In addition to his Thermos, Harold stashed a brown paper bag in the corner of the small table at his position. Unlike the flight mechanic's seat, which faced inward, the radio operator sat facing the outside of the plane, toward a small round window—though radio equipment blocked most of the view. Harold settled into his seat and positioned his notebook, pencil, flight charts, and list of radio frequencies along the route.

Captain Williams and Ed, under the direction of Leonard, went back out and performed the exterior preflight. Jack operated the controls while they checked for correct movement, then they scurried out of the biting wind and back into the plane. The wind and waves rocked the plane from side to side, the swaying motion making it a challenge for the men to set their switches, knobs, and levers.

The engines started one by one, seeming to

protest more than usual in the cold air. They spewed smoke, sputtered, and coughed, but finally settled down into a contented, loping idle, all four sets of propellers turning easily, slowly enough that the blades were visible.

"The weather hasn't worsened much," Captain Williams said, "so we're taking off."

"All right," Leonard said. "Have a good flight. Call us from Miami."

Captain Williams nodded. "We'll do that."

Leonard exited the plane, the wind whipping in through the open hatch before Jack secured it.

Harold had the radios warmed up and had turned on the interphone system so the crew could communicate through the headsets and microphones, rather than talking over the sounds of the four big engines. At the captain's signal, the ground crew untied the securing ropes, and he brought the power up just enough to ease the big plane away from the dock. As they taxied out to the takeoff and landing lane, waves jolted the plane back and forth, growing even larger in the open water. They made the engine checks and a last-minute check of the critical items for takeoff—those things that could prevent the airplane from lifting off or remaining airborne. The captain called out the items, and Jack verified each one: flaps retracted, trim set, propellers set.

Captain Williams then called Ed over the intercom. "Mechanic, temperatures and pressures in the green?"

"All in the green."

The big plane was ready.

The men pulled their safety belts snugly around them.

Captain Williams smoothly advanced the throttles, and the engines increased from idle to the roar of full power, the propellers churning and clawing the air. Unable to face the plane directly into the wind, the captain countered the quartering headwind from the right—which threatened to throw it off course—with control inputs to maintain heading and keep the plane in the channel. The plane picked up speed, the bow lifted slightly, water sprayed from the hull. The waves thudded against the plane, hitting hard enough that the men could hear them over the engine. And they felt them, since each wave sent a shudder throughout the plane. Ed concentrated on the gauges, looking for any variance from normal. The task grew more difficult as the plane shuddered, causing the needles to bounce. Harold clung to his table. Jack called out airspeed, ready, poised to offer any assistance the captain needed on the controls.

The plane plowed through the white-capped waves, gaining speed and throwing the spray of water ever higher until a wall of water engulfed the plane, then it broke free. The wall of water vanished abruptly, and the slapping waves and thundering and shuddering quit. But all was not smooth. The gusting wind created turbulence that rocked the plane side to side and batted it up and down—a rough ride that promised to last for a good while.

As it gained altitude, the plane settled into a steady, rhythmic bounce. After a while, this became soothing, friendly, and the men relaxed and settled in. The course to Miami followed a path that would take them over long stretches of water just off the coast. If they did encounter an emergency and had to set down, the water was welcome, comforting even, as this was a true seaplane with no landing gear, a real flying boat.

The windows that lined the passenger cabin on both sides, and those of the radio and mechanic stations, were round like a ship's portholes. The flight deck sat higher than the passenger cabin, like a ship's bridge, but this ship moved at 150 miles per hour airspeed. At this point, however, the plane experienced a tailwind from the northwest, making the groundspeed 180 miles per hour. Pilots liked tailwinds. So did passengers, even though they were usually unaware—all they knew was that the flight went by quicker than advertised.

"Storm's getting close, captain," Jack said in his slow, easy way, a hint of Missouri drawl sounding in his words. He nodded toward the darkening clouds off to starboard. Gray steaks of rain mixed with snow flowed from the cloud bottoms. "Going to need to change course?"

"Yeah, plot a course that will take us around to the east. We can't get behind the storm; it extends too far west. All we can do is go around the front side and try to outrun it."

Jack left his seat and knelt beside Harold, who had the charts spread out on his table. Jack used the circular slide rule—the whiz wheel—to calculate the speed of the approaching storm and plot where it would be at various times. Then he plotted the plane's speed and where it would be at those same times.

"Captain, we need to divert to the east immediately. If not, we'll catch the center of it over Manhattan."

"Give me a course."

"Yes sir. As soon as I can."

A few moments later, Jack called out, "One hundred and fifteen degrees. Fly heading one-one-five."

Captain Williams gently turned the big plane to its new heading toward less ominous skies, though the clouds were beginning to lower. He opened the throttles for more speed.

"Captain," Ed called.

"Go ahead."

"Number three is beginning to run a little warm."

"Are we all right?"

"For now. I think it may be too lean. I'll richen up the mixture a bit."

"We're going to need all the fuel we've got. Stay as lean as you can."

"Roger."

Ed adjusted the fuel mixture using the controls at his station. As an airplane gains altitude, the amount of fuel flowing into the cylinders must be adjusted for the decreased density of the air to maintain the proper ratio. If adjustments aren't made, too much fuel for the amount of air enters the cylinders, and the engine loses efficiency and power. If the mixture is leaned too much, the engine can run hot, and if it becomes excessively lean, engine damage can result. Ed had to hunt carefully for the correct balance. He made a tiny adjustment, watched the manifold pressure gauge for engine power output, and kept a close eye on cylinder head temperature, then he adjusted another tiny amount, searching for the perfect combination.

The men flew the aircraft toward the middle of the ocean, racing the approaching storm. They watched the dark clouds to their right come closer. Rain pelted from their bottoms at a sharp angle, indicating the fierceness of the wind. Inside the swirling clouds, the winds would be even stronger and could easily send the plane plummeting to earth.

The rain and clouds obscured New York City and the Manhattan skyscrapers, which normally would be visible. The clouds swiftly grew lower, forcing the plane down and back into the turbulent air where it bounced and shook and bucked, making it more difficult for the crew to do their jobs. Jack returned to the copilot's seat to assist the captain, and Harold tried his best to tune the radios, but the plane's violent gyrations made it difficult even to grasp the knobs, let alone turn them accurately. The engine instruments at Ed's station were little more than a blur. The needles bounced continuously, and all he could do was make an estimate of what they really indicated. Jack scanned the gauges and watched the sky, ready to assist if called on.

Captain Williams held the control wheel with firm hands. He worked it left and right to keep the plane level and back and forth to maintain a reasonably constant altitude. His feet worked the rudder pedals continuously, feet dancing and hands turning left and right and back and forth, his jaw set and his gaze unswerving—fighting a battle against the force of the storm.

Rain struck the plane, at first not much more than

a sprinkle, then suddenly, as if flood gates had been thrown open, it hammered against the plane with so much force it could be heard over the sound of the engines and the propellers. The line between sky and ocean vanished in the deluge, and the pilots had to rely on the flight instruments to keep the plane under control. A flash of lightning off to the west lit up the flight deck. Then another flash as the main part of the storm closed in.

Just as suddenly as the rain had begun, it stopped, and the plane broke into clearing sky. The steady hum and rhythm of the engines and propellers filled the cockpit—all that could be heard now that no rain beat against the aluminum fuselage. The clouds lifted, and the sky brightened, the ominous storm disappearing behind the speeding plane.

The captain turned to Jack and said, "Plot a course to Miami."

"Yes sir." Jack got up and once again knelt beside Harold's table while they worked out a path to put the plane back on course.

Once the plane left the turbulent air, Harold lit his pipe. The smoke drifted up and out over the flight deck, filling the air with the aroma of cherry vanilla tobacco.

"Mechanic," Captain Williams said.

"Go ahead."

"How's number three doing?"

"Appears number three is back to normal. Just took some fiddling with the mixture."

"Roger. Good work. And how's the fuel looking for the rest of the trip?"

"At the present rate of flow, we should have enough. But we can't continue off course much longer."

"Roger." The captain insisted they use formal language during flight operations.

Jack returned to his seat. "Set a course for two-two-zero. That should get us back on track for Miami. If we fly this heading for thirty minutes, we should intercept our original course, then we'll make adjustment in heading."

"Roger. Mister Smith, would you like to take the controls?"

"Yes sir, I would."

Jack eased the plane up in a shallow climb toward their normal cruise altitude of six thousand feet. The men settled quietly into their jobs. The excitement of the storm behind them left them drained and contemplative. The air was smooth now, not even any chop, and the blue of the ocean slid by beneath them. The east coast came within their view at times, the land slipping by beyond the starboard wingtip. They'd cross over the outer banks of North Carolina and pass within miles of Kitty Hawk, the hallowed land where powered heavier-than-air flight began. Once this land was behind them, they'd again be over the ocean the remainder of the way to Miami and the Caribbean Airways dock.

But that was over six hours away.

~

The Miami skyline came into view over the nose. The glistening high-rise buildings reached upward in the bright afternoon sun, and the water of the Atlantic Ocean sparkled. Boats, both commercial and small sailing craft, glided smoothly along. Beyond the downtown region, streets stretched out to the west, streets lined with small shops and houses where people went about daily duties while four men in a big, new, shiny airplane sailed toward a landing at Dinner Key Marina.

Dinner Key was the site of a naval training station during the Great War. Through dredging, moving, and filling in of earth, the original island, or key as the locals referred to it, transformed from an island into a peninsula that jutted into Biscayne Bay. After the war, the naval station closed, and the great 1926 hurricane demolished the original buildings. McClelland used Dinner Key as his base for Eastern

South American Airways, then Caribbean Air took it over along with his airline. The name Dinner Key came about due to its preference by locals as a picnic spot.

The Caribbean Airways building—the usual Miami stucco-covered structure with a bit of art deco styling—had large windows that overlooked the docks so waiting passengers could view the planes coming and going, making their graceful water landings and their powerful takeoffs. Just beyond the terminal, sailboats filled the boat marina.

Jack followed the shoreline, past the downtown buildings, and descended lower as the terminal came closer. He turned southeastward, out over the ocean toward Key Biscayne, before turning back toward the terminal, to the landing lane marked by buoys. He lost altitude as he did so to capture the correct glide path down to the water.

After securing the plane, the men, overnight bags in hand, caught a cab for the US Hotel located downtown across the street from the Florida East Coast Railway station. The thirty-five-room hotel, a two-story, light-colored stone building, had green-and-white striped canvas awnings on second-floor windows and a green metal awning along the front on the first floor. It'd had a speakeasy in an upstairs room during prohibition, but when the Prohibition

Act was repealed, it reverted to an ordinary hotel room. Captain Williams and Jack shared a room, and Ed and Harold shared another.

"Headin' out to see Jennifer?" Jack asked.

"Going to clean up a bit and head to her place right away. She'll be home from teaching about the time I get there."

"She'll be surprised."

"A little. She knows we were due in today. So how 'bout your evening?"

"I'll go out later and grab a bite, then turn in early."

"Going to Wong's?"

"Yeah."

"Seeing Sally?"

"Hope so. Hope she's working this evening."

A short while later, Captain Williams emerged from the bathroom dressed in a gray suit, shiny black wingtip shoes, and a dark red necktie, his mustache trimmed and hair combed—a dapper image. Jack also cleaned up and changed clothes, exchanging his Caribbean Airways uniform for a dark suit. He looked in the long mirror on the inside of the bathroom door, noted a corner of his shirttail pulling loose, and tucked it in. Try as he could, he lacked the sharp image of Captain Williams.

Wong's Chop Suey Palace was the favorite place to eat for Jack and Captain Williams when they were in Miami. They visited four times a week while their scheduled flight to Nassau waited three hours for mail and freight to arrive by East Coast Airlines. They used some of the time to go to lunch, taking a cab downtown and arriving at Wong's at opening time, 11a.m.

The restaurant sat just a block from the hotel on the same side of the street. Its sign, visible from the bustling train depot, called people for exotic dining, something different than the traditional meat and potatoes of the standard American fare. The single-story stucco building, the stucco tinged slightly pink, featured a green pagoda roof awning above the front entrance. A neon sign in the window declared "Open," and above that in bigger, bolder letters, also in neon, "Wong's Chop Suey Palace" glowed softly. As soon as a person stepped through the door, the smell of exotic cuisine overcame the senses—the fragrances of anise, fennel seed, clove, cinnamon, and soy sauce, as well as cooking beef, chicken, bok choy, celery, onions, and garlic. Jack's mouth watered instantly.

Tables and chairs lined the walls, and a couple of larger tables occupied the area in the middle of the room. Scenes from the Orient—woods, pagodas, and bamboo forests—covered the lower eighteen inches of the windows. A paper dragon hung from the ceiling.

Charlie Wong himself was as much an institution as the restaurant. A kindly, polite man, he wore a traditional changshan—a shirt with exposed buttons up the front, high collar, and long, wide sleeves—and his eyes sparkled and danced behind gold-rimmed glasses. He flitted about the room in a blur, going from table to table, chatting and joking with each customer.

He manned the cash register himself and profusely thanked each patron, handing them a small box of Chiclets gum as they headed out the door, then he scurried off to greet and chat with more customers.

Charlie's wife, June, kept order in the kitchen, directing the cooks and waitstaff in her calm, quiet, yet firm manner, and their son, Walter, worked in the kitchen, sweating and chopping and dicing and stirring. Daughter Sally waited tables and helped in the kitchen, whatever task needed her at any moment. She wore the typical waitress uniform of the day—a dark red, mid-calf-length dress with white collar and cuffs on the short sleeves and a white apron tied about her waist. She wore her long, black hair pinned up and moved swiftly yet gracefully from table to table, order pad and pencil in hand, taking orders and meeting customers' requests for more tea, coffee, or water.

Charlie and June's story was one of determination and hard work. They had met and married in their home city of Shanghai before immigrating to America. Immigration had been difficult for Chinese people due to the Chinese Exclusion Act passed by congress in 1882. The act prohibited Chinese laborers from immigrating for ten years, and it required Chinese people in the United States to carry certification papers that identified their occupation. After the initial ten-year period, the Exclusion Act was extended, though eventually the federal government left it up to individual states to enforce it. The western states enforced the act while the eastern states took a more relaxed attitude. Thus, Asian immigrants arrived alongside European immigrants as they processed through Ellis Island. This is where Zhang Yong and Wang Yan arrived in America and began their lives as Charlie and June Wong. After working in June's uncle's restaurant in New York City, they migrated to Miami to make it on their own and to escape the bitter northeastern winters. Though difficult and slow going at first, the business now thrived, the room full at mealtimes.

When Jack had first laid eyes on Sally, he'd fallen head over heels for her, captivated by her exotic looks, her dark eyes and black hair. When she talked with him, he fell even deeper. Their conversation quickly became comfortable, as if he'd known her forever. Jack, normally nervous meeting a woman, felt at ease with this girl with her kind manner and gentle nature. That had been a month ago, on Jack's first flight on the route with Captain Williams.

After only a couple of visits to the restaurant, Jack and Sally's conversations lengthened, sometimes to the point where her father had to remind her, by a look or a command, to tend to other customers. Captain Williams got to excusing himself after the meal so Jack could have all Sally's attention when she brought the check. Jack wanted to get to know this girl better, ask her for a date, but thus far courage had fallen a bit short.

Jack walked toward Wong's neon sign. It glowed in the fading evening light, sending out a soft electric message that beckoned people to step inside. He arrived after the evening crowd had gone, in the lull that existed before the later crowd poured in after movies and other entertainment. The restaurant was quiet, only three or four customers lingering over their food, chatting and laughing.

Charlie Wong greeted him warmly. "Good evening, Mister Jack. It's unusual to see you here this time of day. A different flight?"

"Yes, we just returned from Stratford, Connecticut, and we're overnighting here before heading to Nassau in the morning. We ferried in a new airplane."

"A new airplane? Does this mean business is growing?"

"Yes, it does. We're expanding our route system, and this new plane can get us farther into South America."

"Yes, considerable expansion. Is Captain Max and his lady friend Miss Jennifer going to join you?"

"They may be along later; I really don't know. So a table for one will do."

"Right this way, Mister Jack. Sally will be along in a moment to wait on you."

"Thank you, Charlie."

Sally walked up to Jack's table as soon as Charlie had seated him. "Good evening, Jack. It's a nice surprise to see you this time of day." She looked down briefly, then asked, "How are you this evening?"

"Oh, very well. And you?"

"The same; very well. I think I overheard you and Father talking about a new airplane, one you flew from Connecticut."

"Yes. We ferried down a brand-new airplane today. Had a little rough weather around New York City, but once clear of that, it was a great trip. The new plane has four engines and is the biggest plane I've ever flown. Oh, Sally, I don't mean to go on."

"Please continue, Jack. I think it's interesting.

It's hard to imagine that you left Connecticut this morning and are eating an evening meal in Miami. The world is really changing."

"Yes, it is. Good or bad, it's getting smaller thanks in part to the airplane. This new plane cruises at 150 miles per hour so that really shrinks distances. We're going to fly it to South America, all the way to Buenos Aires."

"That sounds so exciting."

"It should be. I'm looking forward to it."

"Do you know when you're leaving?" she asked.

"Not for sure, but it'll be soon. The plane's going to need some modifications for the survey flight. The interior is going to be stripped out and a temporary navigator's station put in. You should see the plane now, it's really nice inside. Wood paneled walls, thick seats, and tables that fold down for dining, all first-class. It really will be luxury traveling." Jack paused, then asked, "Ever been up in a plane?"

"No."

"Would you like to?"

"I would. But I can't afford a ticket. Traveling by airplane is for rich people."

Feeling a burst of courage, Jack said, "I was thinking, I could take you up in a small plane. Rent a two-seater plane and take you out over the city and down along the coast."

Sally looked away and blushed. Looking back at Jack, she replied, "I'd like that."

It was Jack's turn to blush.

After a bit of awkward silence, Sally asked, "Your usual tonight?"

"Yeah, yes, my usual. You know my usual?"

"Of course. Beef chop suey, two spring rolls, iced tea."

As Sally headed toward the kitchen, Jack unfolded his napkin slowly. The cloth was the same dark red as Sally's dress, and he played with one corner of it, absently bending it over and back, his mind deep in thought.

Jack was finishing his meal when Charlie greeted Captain Williams and Jennifer as they entered the restaurant. Unable to see Jack, who faced away from the entrance, they took a table to themselves. After waiting on them, Sally returned to Jack's table.

"How are your college classes going?" Jack asked.

"Classes are going well; I'm maintaining perfect grades so far, but that could change. One class is particularly difficult, and the professor is tough, but I'll get through it."

"I know you will; you're a smart person. Math is your area of study, isn't it?"

"It is."

"So what are your plans after college?"

"I hope to be a teacher, a high school math teacher.

I dream someday of getting an advanced degree and teaching college. That's what I really want to do."

"Math is something that doesn't come naturally for me. I respect anyone who is good at it."

"Don't you use math in flying?"

"Some, but it's pretty basic unless you get into the science of aerodynamics, and I'm not an engineer."

Charlie called for Sally.

"I'll see you after your trip, Jack," she said before hurrying into the back room. "Be safe."

On his way out, Jack spotted the captain and Jennifer. She wore a yellow day dress and no hat. The large, soft curls of her long, brown hair fell over her shoulders.

He stopped at their table. "Well, good evening, you two."

After exchanging greetings, Jennifer asked if he wanted to sit and visit for a while.

"Aw, no thank you. I need to get going."

"Have a nice visit with Sally?" the captain asked.

"I sure did." Jack couldn't suppress a grin. "I'll see you later. Good to see you, Jennifer. Enjoy the evening." Jack headed out the door into the warm evening, an extra spring in his step.

~

When Captain Williams returned to the hotel, Jack was still up, reading, or at least pretending to read, but it was obvious his mind was many miles away. "Well, how was your evening with Jennifer?" he asked.

"Very nice. We took in a good movie, caught the early show, before eating at Wong's. And good news! She got the teaching job in Nassau. She's beginning with summer session."

"That's great! You won't have to travel to Miami to see her."

"Indeed. I'm looking forward to it. And you seem in quite a good mood."

"I suppose I am."

"So you had a nice conversation with Sally?"

"I did."

After a bit of silence, Captain Williams asked, "Well, aren't you going to tell me more?"

"More? You think there's more?"

"Of course. It's written all over your face."

"Actually, there's not a lot more."

"You can't fool me, Jack Smith! I know good and well there's more that you haven't told me."

Jack reiterated the conversation with Sally, including the part about taking her flying.

A knock came at the door. "Yes?" Captain Williams asked.

"Harold."

"Come on in."

"Just wanted to check on tomorrow's plans," Harold said, the smoke from his pipe drifting about his face. "What time we plan to leave?"

"We'll make it a leisurely morning," the captain replied. "Take off about nine o'clock. Be at the dock by eight. You and Ed join us for breakfast, if you like. By the way, where is your roommate?"

"I have no idea and don't really care." Harold left abruptly.

Jack frowned. "What do you think of him?"

"He seems to know his radios."

"Yeah, but what do you think of his personality?"

The captain shrugged. "He's a bit aloof." After a pause to think, he added, "But maybe he's just shy, uncomfortable in new surroundings."

"Think he'll cause any problems?"

"I don't think so. Nothing serious, anyway."

"Hope you're right."

Dust Storm

In the United States, out of the Oklahoma Panhandle, a storm built and swirled in the spring winds of the Great Plains. The winds normally carried in a new growing season, but now they swept away all hope of a new crop as the sky blackened with the wind carrying away the nutrient-providing topsoil. The wind carried the soil high into the heavens and eastward to Chicago where it deposited twelve million pounds of topsoil on the city. The remaining soil found its way on to Cleveland, Buffalo, and finally to Washington, DC.

Following the Great War, wheat was like gold as demand for it skyrocketed. Farmers flocked to the Great Plains and, with fire-breathing machinery, giant tractors, and wide plows, turned under the natural prairie grass and went to work feeding the hungry nation. The depression killed the lucrative market and then, right on the heels of the fallen economy, a drought hit the Great Plains, and the overworked and over-plowed land turned to powder.

The great dust blizzard scoured the landscape and the houses, fences, cars, and windmills. It cracked and popped with blue discharges of static electricity. Dust infiltrated everything, finding its way in through microscopic cracks in homes and businesses, and deep into lungs. Jackrabbits and grasshoppers invaded the parched plains. The breadbasket of the nation became the biblical plague of the nation.

Chapter Three

Nassau, a city of twenty thousand people, mixed old and new. Two-wheeled carts shared the streets with Ford Model As, and workaday Bahamians went about their business while white European and American travelers, dressed in their finery, looked on.

These tourists, relatively unaffected by the worldwide depression, traveled by air and ship. After conversion, ships that had been used as transports became luxury oceangoing hotels with the finest of amenities that transformed an arduous voyage across the Atlantic into a glamorous experience.

"Getting there is half the fun!" declared an ad from the Cunard Line enticing wealthy Europeans to cross the cold ocean waters to revel in a tropical paradise. United States travelers had the option to travel by air, and they did so on Caribbean Airways, whose flights went to many of the far-flung islands dotting the Caribbean Sea.

Guides herded the wealthy foreigners throughout the city to view the historic buildings, the colonial architecture, and the Christ Church Cathedral with its famous tower, and encouraged them to buy souvenirs from the shops on Bay Street, the main shopping area. Tourists gazed in wonder at the sponge market and the Bahamians trimming and preparing the sponges. All while the Bahamians pushed their two-wheeled carts and drove their horse-drawn wagons about the narrow streets, hustling to and from market to scratch out a meager daily living.

Just months before, due to prohibition in the United States, Nassau boomed from the bootleg alcohol business. When that cash cow died December 5, 1933, tourism suddenly became vital.

Jack flew the plane over the familiar stretch of water between Miami and Nassau, while Captain Williams relaxed, but he still scanned the sky and the aircraft gauges as Jack's backup. As Nassau neared, Jack reduced power and allowed the plane to make a gentle descent. Ed adjusted fuel mixtures and kept an eye on the engine instruments. Harold had long ago tuned in to the Nassau frequency. Communications between the base and those Caribbean Airways planes crisscrossing the warm tropical skies occasionally interrupted the static background.

Caribbean Airways, the first airline to employ ground-to-air communications, touted this safety feature in their advertising. A soothing female voice with a Jamaican accent provided sweet contrast to the harsh male voices that stated aircraft position, estimated arrival times, and requests for wind reports and weather updates. The voice belonged to Vivian Liverpool, a Jamaican now living in Nassau and working the radio communication for the airline.

The pilots did a flyover of the city and docks to announce the arrival of the new airplane. The rumble of the big engines sounded different than the twin-engine planes with which people were familiar, causing them to pause and peer upward where, for a brief moment, the big aircraft blocked the sun from view. Jack prepared for landing in the water between New Providence Island and the much smaller Paradise Island. This naturally protected stretch of water harbored ships as well as the seaplanes.

When the New Providence dock and the Caribbean Airways terminal, built on the water's edge, came into view, Jack exclaimed, "Look down there! Look at all those people."

People filled the shoreline, standing shoulder to shoulder, all with heads turned upward, hands shading eyes from the brilliant sun as they watched the silver airplane soar gracefully overhead. Jack flew out toward open water and then turned onto final approach, the plane gradually descending, wing flaps fully extended. The engine power reduced and the plane touched down in a giant spray of water. It slowed and turned toward the new dock built specifically for this much larger airplane.

"What are all those people doing?" Ed asked through the intercom. "Hey, looks like they're waving."

Jack grinned. "They are."

He and the captain slid open their side windows and waved in return to the crowd who cheered so loudly that the men could hear them over the rumble of the idling engines. As the plane approached the dock, the men had to forgo their waving to attend to the delicate job of getting the big plane into position. Passengers just getting off an S-38 turned to watch. The plane settled into position, and the ground crew hustled to fasten the securing ropes. One by one, the big engines shuddered to a stop.

Captain Williams peered out the window. "Fellas, I think I see news photographers. We'll do our postflight check and make sure the plane is secured. Then we'll exit together and stay close. No doubt there's reporters there too. Don't let them separate us. And act pleasant. Smile."

Ed snorted. "Smile, my foot!"

"Mister Butz, you're representing the airline!"

Ed just grumbled and clamped his cigar tighter. Harold looked panicked.

Once the plane was secure, the four men stepped into the bright sunlight. Cheering, applause, and the snapping of photographers' cameras met them on shore. Jack and the captain smiled and waved. Ed chewed on his cigar, flashing an occasional half-hearted wave, and Harold looked down, his pipe clenched in the corner of his mouth. Half a dozen news reporters surged forward.

"Captain Williams! What do you think of the new plane?" one of them shouted, trying to be heard over all the cheering and clapping.

"Yes, what do you think?" shouted another.

Captain Williams smiled. "We won't make any comments now. But if you meet us inside in a few minutes, we'll answer any questions."

He led the men up the ramp and toward the terminal, the throng of people still cheering and straining to get a look at the men who'd maneuvered this big machine from the sky and into the harbor. It surely took a special kind of person to fly a plane. Charles Lindbergh, Jimmy Doolittle, and Roscoe Turner were men of special talent and ability, as were the women pilots, including Ruth Elder, Louise

Thadden, and Bessie Coleman. People couldn't get enough of them, these heroes of the sky. The four men walking up the ramp were of this special breed; to stand near them, cheer for them, was an honor.

Inside, some of the ground crew stood guard at the foot of the steps that led to the second floor of the terminal. They stepped aside to let the crew up, then moved back into position across the stairs to hold back the reporters and curious folks.

The captain stepped into the terminal manager's office.

"What's the crowd all about?" Captain Williams asked Don Wilcox, the manager. "I assume it's because of the new plane, but why so many people? You should've warned us."

"I had no idea it would be this big," Wilcox, a stocky, disheveled, middle-aged man replied. Gray peppered his curly brown hair, and a perpetual cigarette with a long ash dangled from the corner of his mouth. He wore no coat or tie, and his wrinkled white shirt was half in, half out of the waistband of his dark pants. "It's part of the publicity the old man wants. We figured there'd be the reporters and photographers, maybe a handful of other folks that would show up, but nothing like this."

Ed and Harold wandered into the conference room to await the reporters. Jack ambled into the communications room.

Vivian swiveled her chair around from the radio. "Good morning, Mister Jack." She wore a bright red and white head tie and a smile as big as her personality. Her print dress, ankle-length and full, featured large flowers in red, yellow, and purple.

"Good morning, Vivian. How are you today?"

"Well, Mister Jack, very well. And you?"

"The same; couldn't be better."

Gail Rogers, another communications woman, turned toward Jack after finishing a radio transmission. "It looks like you fellas are famous."

Gail, a short woman in her mid twenties, wore black-framed glasses and her chestnut-brown hair styled in a long, side-parted bob. She normally wore mid-calf-length day dresses and favored wide belts, large collars, puff sleeves, and polka dots. Cold midwestern winters and a broken relationship that left her as empty as the windswept plains had brought her to Nassau, and she'd been with Caribbean Airways just a few weeks less than Jack.

Jack chuckled. "Aw, I don't think it's us. It's the airplane. We just happened to be the ones in it."

"We got to see you come in. When you announced you were five miles out, Don let Vivian and I go into his office to watch out the window. It was quite a sight to see you come in on approach. Were you flying?"

"Actually, I was. The captain had me fly the entire leg this morning from takeoff to landing."

She smiled. "He has confidence in you."

"I guess he must."

Normally the flight captain did the flying with the first officer there to assist. But Captain Williams encouraged his copilots to fly as often as possible, especially the ones he sensed had good skills and judgment. He'd hinted to Jack that he'd make captain soon.

"Gail, I better get back with the crew. I think the press wants to talk with us."

"Bye, Jack. Maybe I'll see you later."

"Maybe."

The four crewmen along with Wilcox gathered in the conference room, and then they allowed the press upstairs. They thundered up the steps, notebooks poised, cameras loaded.

Questions poured forth, most of them directed at Captain Williams, who projected confidence and optimism with just a bit of pilot swagger, though he emphasized that Jack had flown in and made the landing, and he pointed out that Ed and Harold were also important members of the crew. Don Wilcox interjected to emphasize a point and act important, reminding the reporters of his position as terminal manager. Flashbulbs lit up the room, going off in such rapid succession that it was as if a steady, blazing light filled the room.

Then it was over.

The room was suddenly quiet. Empty. The men sat for a moment as if stunned. Then Captain Williams spoke, giving the cue to get up, leave the room, and get on with their lives. "Fellas, we have work to do."

The men quietly left and made their way through the terminal, still now except for a few lingering people. On the way to the dock as they passed through the lobby, the men noted the new restaurant that had opened while they were away.

The restaurant, located within the terminal, offered views of the harbor through the panoramic windows that lined the outside wall. Patrons could watch boats and seaplanes as they traveled in and out. The terminal itself was a gleaming white stucco, two-story building with a red tile roof and abundant windows. Outside, palm trees stood watch, swaying in the tropical breeze.

The maintenance and storage buildings sat across the street that ran behind the terminal. Though much of the maintenance happened when a plane was at its dock, when extensive work was needed, the mechanics towed planes on dollies up a ramp from the water's edge and across the street to the maintenance hangar—a white block building with a high arching roof.

Inside the restaurant, a handful of patrons—some Caribbean Airways passengers and employees, others local businesspeople—sat scattered here and there at tables covered with white linen tablecloths and set with fine china. A couple of waiters dressed in white jackets took orders and served food. In back, behind the double swinging doors, the cooks prepared the food under the direction of the head chef, a Caribbean native who'd studied in Paris, where he perfected his natural ability for creating fine cuisine.

"Business looks a bit slow in there," Jack said.

Ed nodded. "Yeah, it does. Hope it picks up for them." Then, addressing the captain, he said, "I need to get something out of the plane, out of the baggage compartment."

"All right, go ahead."

"I know I should have told you about this before, but I didn't."

"What have you got stashed away?"

"Let me get it."

Outdoors, all was back to normal, the mass of people having dispersed, going back to homes and work, resuming normal lives. Ed sauntered down to the plane, and the other three men followed. He entered the aircraft through the passenger door and reappeared shortly after at the crew door, wrestling a motorcycle out onto the dock.

Captain Williams's eyebrows shot up. "Butz! Where'd you get that?"

"A motorcycle!" Jack exclaimed. "Ol' Butz can come up with anything."

"I put it aboard in Miami last night. Got a great deal on it. Runs too."

Jack appraised the bike. "So what have you got there, Ed?"

"An Indian."

He nodded. "I'd like to have a cycle someday. Sure be handy for getting around the island."

"Maybe we can work a deal."

"Not now," the captain said. "Get that thing put away in the maintenance hangar, and I'll meet you up there in a bit."

Ed climbed on the motorcycle, pumped the throttle, and kicked the starter. The machine fired on the first kick, belching smoke briefly. He blipped the throttle a couple of times, then rode the machine up the ramp and across the road.

Harold shook his head. "Huh. I'm not sure if I believe it. Wonder who he conned to get it? And how'd he get it aboard?"

"We don't ask," Jack said. "He won't give you a straight answer, anyway."

Captain Williams tossed a set of car keys to Jack. "I've got paperwork to do. Take my car and take Harold to the New Colonial. Stop for groceries or whatever he needs, and show him around the island." He turned to Harold and continued, "The company's putting you up until you get a place. The New Colonial is a nice place, first-class hotel. We'll send a car for you in the morning."

Jack helped Harold with his bags and loaded them in the captain's car, a 1932 Ford Model B coupe, Washington Blue with black fenders and running boards.

Ed and Captain Williams stood in the immense doorway of the maintenance hangar, discussing the temporary navigator's station in the new plane.

"Do we have a navigator?" Ed asked.

The captain nodded. "The old man lined up one for us. He's to be here tomorrow. Lyle Ellison."

"Ellison the drunk! The old man outta his mind?" Ed pulled the cigar out of the corner of his mouth and spat on the ground. "Ellison went on a bender and ended up getting that crew lost in North Africa. He's the only one who survived."

"Yeah, I know. At least, that's the story. He's

definitely had some problems in the past, but the old man assures me that's all behind him. He did give me the authority to kick him off the crew no matter where we are if there's problems. He is a good navigator, maybe the best."

"When he's sober," Ed said.

"Careful, Mister Butz."

"I was never drunk while on duty in Europe, and I've never been drunk at Caribbean Air."

"Good. Keep it that way."

~

The next day, Jack and Captain Williams rode as passengers on the daily flight to Miami, both on a mission to see their girls before leaving on the survey flight. For the captain, a date with Jennifer was a sure thing; for Jack, a chance to see Sally wasn't certain, but he was willing to take the chance.

"So what are you and Jennifer going to do?" Jack asked as the two sat back in the passenger cabin of the S-38.

"Go out for a nice meal, then take in a show. *The Thin Man.* That's the name of the show. Supposed to be funny. Hope she enjoys it. What are your plans? Going to set up a date with Sally?"

"Well, I hope so. We have kind of talked about

me taking her up in a plane. So I decided before we leave, I'd better make a definite date, you know, a movie and a meal out, a nice time. I hope she's working tonight, kinda taking a chance, but maybe I can call her at home if she's off. I think her father will give me the number."

The captain smiled. "I hope it all works out."

~

After checking in at the US Hotel, Captain Max Williams went to visit Jennifer Connors, walking the dozen blocks from the hotel to her apartment. She lived on a street that lay in the zone that faded from commercial to residential, from storefronts and facades to modest single-family houses, the familiar bungalows of Miami. Apartment buildings peppered this in-between zone, this buffer between business and residential. Jennifer's building was a two-story, stucco-covered affair, off-white with concrete steps leading up to a foyer lined with dark wood. Multipaned windows, one on each side of the doorway, offered a view out over the sidewalk and the street. Inside, two doors on each side of the hallway led to four apartments. The same pattern repeated on the second floor where Jennifer lived.

Captain Williams knocked on the door of

number twenty-two. No answer. He knocked again, then listened for activity from within. Nothing. He wandered back downstairs and out into the sunshine, then sat on the front steps to wait.

Some children passed by—skipping, running, laughing, schoolbooks in hand—signaling that school had let out for the day. A woman walking a small dog—some variety of poodle—ambled by in the opposite direction. A woman with bright red lipstick and long blonde hair, wearing dark blue, wide-legged, high-waist trousers and a nautical-themed blouse, came up the steps. Captain Williams acknowledged her with a nod.

"Say, mister, you must be waitin' on someone," she said while chomping on chewing gum.

"Yes, ma'am."

"Who? Maybe I can help you."

"Jennifer Connors. The schoolteacher."

"Oh, you must be the pilot. She said she was expectin' you today. She should be along any minute. She usually gets home about this time every day, that is, unless there's some special activity at the school. But she didn't say nothin' about that for today. My name's Marla, by the way, just moved in a few weeks ago."

"Nice to meet you, Marla." Captain Williams stood up to formally acknowledge her. "My name's

Max Williams."

"Oh sweetie, there's no need to stand up. I'm pretty informal."

"So you know Jennifer well?"

"We both live on the second floor. We pass comin' and goin' and stop and visit. Chitchat, that kind of thing. Of course, bein' girls, we talk about men, and she told me about you. I'm envious. And, honey, I'm really envious now that I've met you."

The captain blushed a bit and made no response. Then he asked, "Jennifer will be right along, you say?"

"Aw, she should be. She is a bit late, though. Must've had something unexpected after school let out, maybe helpin' a kid with some schoolwork. She's good at that, you know, helpin' kids. She wants to see them learn; do real good. She's a good teacher."

"She enjoys it a lot, and she seems to have a way with the kids. I've heard her talk about students who've struggled, and then done particularly well. That makes her feel good."

"Max!" a voice called out.

Captain Williams turned to see Jennifer hurrying toward him, purse over one shoulder and a satchel in one hand, her navy blue polka dot dress fluttering as she ran. Captain Williams bounded down the steps to meet her. She dropped the satchel. They threw their arms around each other, and he picked her off the ground and swung her around.

"You most certainly look nice," he said, stepping back to take her all in.

"And you look quite nice yourself." Then she noticed Marla standing on the steps, a grin on her face. "Isn't he swell!" Jennifer exclaimed.

"My, you are a lucky woman," she responded. "I'll leave you two be." Marla started up the steps, stopped and turned back to the captain and said, "Say, if you have any friends who are unattached, let me know." Then she disappeared into the building.

"Did she talk you to death?"

"No. But she is a character, isn't she?"

~

Later in the evening, after the dinner hour, Jack walked the couple of blocks from the hotel to Wong's. As he approached the front door, he saw Sally through the windows hustling about cleaning tables and checking on the few lingering customers.

Charlie greeted him. "Good evening, Mister Jack. How are you this fine evening?"

"Very well, Charlie. Couldn't be better."

"Another flight in the new airplane?"

"No, a personal trip. Came over with Captain Williams. He came to see his girl, you know, Jennifer, before we head to South America."

"I see. Will Captain Max and Miss Jennifer be joining you?"

"No, they're at a movie. I'm here alone."

"Well, your usual table is empty. Go ahead and have a seat, and Sally will be with you shortly."

Jack took his place at the table in the far corner and had no more than sat down when Sally greeted him. But something was different, her demeaner distant, all business, the conversation stilted and to the point.

"Sally, are you all right?"

"Fine, I'm fine."

"Something seems to be bothering you."

"No, there's nothing bothering me. I'm just busy tonight."

Jack looked around the room and saw some people lingering at one table.

"I'm busy in the back, in the kitchen," Sally said.

"I see."

"The usual?"

"Yes, that will be fine."

Then she abruptly turned and went toward the kitchen.

When she returned with the food, she said, "Jack, forgive me, but I can't talk. Please. I'm sorry." She hurried off to the back room.

Jack saw the back door swing open and Sally step outside. He ate in silence, his appetite gone, the food that was always so good now tasteless.

After he finished his meal, Charlie came by with the check and asked how he'd enjoyed the food. Jack lied, saying he'd enjoyed it a lot. Charlie, as usual, thanked him profusely and gave him the twin-pack of Chiclets.

Jack walked outside into the humid evening and wandered back to the hotel, his head hanging, hands thrust deep in his pockets. But he couldn't sit and stare at the walls with all that was on his mind, so he decided to take in a movie. He chose *The Count of Monte Cristo*, an adventure film that would help him escape the events of the evening.

After the show, he found his way back to the hotel and lingered in the lobby, watching the people come and go. No matter what, he couldn't take his mind off his bewildering encounter with Sally. He speculated, but couldn't come up with a valid reason for her actions. What could he have done to upset her? To cause her to have such a reversal of attitude? Then he remembered; she'd said, "Forgive me, but I can't talk. Please. I'm sorry." She couldn't talk. Not that she didn't want to, but she couldn't.

Jack turned those words over and over in his mind and said them to himself, emphasizing a different word each time and mixing around the order, but he still he couldn't figure out what had happened. The month he'd known her had been bliss up to this point. He'd learned that she was attending college, paying her own way from her restaurant wages, taking classes only as she could afford them and, at twenty-four years old, still had at least one more year to go. Jack admired her for her determination, her intelligence, and her work ethic. But now it seemed that he had to forget her.

Meanwhile, after their evening out, Captain Williams walked Jennifer to her apartment and said good night, and goodbye for an unknown period of time, the future uncertain. After the final goodbyes and hugs, Jennifer gently closed the door.

As Captain Williams turned to leave, the door to another apartment opened, and a familiar figure stepped out into the hallway. "Butz? What are you doing here?" the captain asked. "Marla?"

Butz grinned. "Yes."

"How?"

"Never you mind."

When the captain returned to the hotel, he found Jack lying awake, fully dressed, on the bed with his arms folded behind his head, staring at the wooden blades of the ceiling fan as they slowly turned.

"So how was your evening at Wong's?" he asked.

"Have a nice conversation with Sally?"

"No, I didn't."

"She wasn't there?"

"Oh, she was there all right, but she gave me the cold shoulder. I don't know why." Jack related the bewildering events while Captain Williams listened.

He neither agreed nor disagreed with Jack, just let him talk and work it all out. After Jack had finished, the captain turned the conversation to the upcoming survey flight and the plans, uncertainties, and adventure with which they'd be faced.

But Jack couldn't forget. He abruptly announced, "I'm going back to Wong's. I have to know what's going on."

Once again Charlie greeted him. "Mister Jack, back already?"

"Yes sir, I am."

"Did you forget something?"

"As a matter of fact, I did."

"Oh?"

"Yes, I want to talk with Sally. I have something I need to say, and I didn't have the chance earlier."

"Mister Jack, I'm afraid Sally is busy right now. We'll be closing in half an hour."

Jack looked around the empty restaurant.

The smile disappeared from Charlie Wong's face.

"Mister Wong, I respect you," Jack said, "but I

really must talk with Sally. I won't be back for three or four weeks, and I'm leaving in two days. I must see her before I go."

Sally appeared and said, "Father, please let me talk to Jack. I need to tell him."

"All right, as you wish. But you be sure to tell him."

"Jack," Sally said, "let's go outside." She led the way through the back room, out the back door, and into the alley and the still, humid night.

"I like you, Jack," she said, "and that's the problem. See, I've been seeing a fella for quite a while. He works as a bookkeeper at his father's business, and my folks like him, and they know his family. And he's Chinese, Chinese American like me. Everyone expects us to get married, and they're getting impatient. I've been dragging my feet, putting off a wedding, but I agreed we'd get married this summer. Everything is in order, nice and tidy, the way it's supposed to be."

Jack's eyes widened. "An arranged marriage?"

"It might as well be."

He frowned. "Are you happy?"

Sally looked away, paused, then said, "I guess I am. I'm supposed to be."

"But are you really?"

She faced him again. "Jack, I don't want to talk about it anymore. You and I, we're just friends, Jack, that's all we can be." She wiped her eyes and looked away again.

Jack said nothing. The two of them stood awkwardly, not looking at each other, until Sally broke the silence. "Jack," she said softly, "tell me again what it's like to fly. Is it peaceful up there in the sky?"

He nodded. "Most of the time it is. If the weather's bad, that's a different story. But late afternoon or early morning, the air is calm, and it's peaceful as can be. The world looks so different from up there. I can't really describe it. A person really has to experience it to understand."

"Have you always wanted to fly?"

"I grew up on a farm in Missouri. The first time I saw an airplane fly over, I knew I had to learn how to fly. There's not a lot of money to be made on a farm in the hills of Missouri, so I joined the air service to learn flying. Spent eight years in it and got to do a lot of flying. I think I told you I even flew down to Panama City and served there for a while at France Field, so I'm no stranger to the Caribbean region."

"Do you plan to always be a pilot?"

"Right now I don't know of anything I'd rather do. The money is pretty good, and I enjoy what I'm doing. I can't imagine doing anything but flying. And I feel fortunate to have a good job in these times. You know the depression has hit so many people hard."

"I know. We're fortunate here too. The restaurant

is doing well thanks to my parents' hard work, and there's enough travelers and businesspeople to keep us busy. Anna May Wong ate here once, so that got us some publicity. This depression won't go on forever—it can't—but for the time being it's difficult for so many."

"Anna May Wong, the actress? She was in your restaurant?"

Sally smiled. "She was, and I even got to meet her. She's no relation, you know. Wong is like Smith is in this country."

"Yeah, there must be at least a thousand guys named Jack Smith. Anyway, the depression, I send money home to my folks back in Missouri. They're having a hard time of it, but at least being on a farm they grow a lot of their own food."

"That's a kind thing to do."

"I can't imagine not doing it." After a pause, Jack said, "Sally, thank you for explaining things to me. I feel better, but I'd be lying if I said wasn't disappointed."

She nodded. "I don't want to hurt you, and I know I did earlier. I'm sorry, but I just didn't know what to do. I was told I was too friendly with you and was reminded that I had a boyfriend."

"Your parents told you that, didn't they?"

"Yes."

Jack sighed. "I respect your parents, and I don't want to come between you and them. And I don't want to cause trouble. But, Sally, I don't know if … well, I don't know if I'll come here anymore to eat. I'm not sure, but I don't think I can. Seeing you, well…"

Sally suddenly threw her arms around him. "You be careful on that long flight. I'll worry about you. And I'll miss you so much."

"We'll be fine."

"Goodbye, Jack," she said quietly.

"Goodbye, Sally."

Jack walked around the outside of the restaurant to the sidewalk, leaving Sally standing in the darkness.

Celluloid Escape

The couple looked deeply and longingly into each other's eyes, then embraced and kissed. Music sounded, and behind them, dancers leaped about a bubbling water fountain. The scene faded out, and the audience left with images of hope for the future, a return to a better time. For twenty-five cents or less, people could escape their drab, desperate lives and through the big screen live vicariously the actors' carefree lives without the worry of income, food, or clothes.

If a few extra pennies could be scraped together, people—individually, in couples, or families—made their way to the nearest movie theater to spend a couple of hours lost in a world so different than their own. The theater doors, once closed and the film began to roll inside the darkened room, shut out the world and its harsh reality.

Cary Grant and Claudette Colbert proceeded to yuk it up in the slapstick, screwball comedy *It Happened One Night*. *Frankenstein* and *Dracula* scared people in a different way than the depression scared them. John Wayne rode his horse off into the sunset, representing a tough, rugged attitude—the same attitude needed to weather the rough-and-tumble economy. James Cagney and Edward G. Robinson opened fire as they blazed their way across the country evading the law.

By scraping together a few cents once a week or once a month, people could leave harsh reality behind for a couple of hours.

Chapter Four

A red beacon flashed on, and from deep within the plane came an electrical hum. The propeller on number one engine jerked to life, turning uncertainly and hesitantly. Smoke billowed from the engine's exhaust. A few cylinders fired, and smoke and flame came in spurts, timed with each firing. The engine sputtered, protesting, then abruptly hit on all cylinders. It roared to life, shattering the early morning calm, then slowed to a loping, soothing idle, the big, three-blade propeller turning slowly. The sequence followed three more times until all four engines idled easily, rocking the plane gently, rhythmically.

At Captain Williams's signal, the ground crew freed the ropes and the plane eased slowly to the takeoff channel. The flight crew made checks as they went, revving up each engine one at a time to test its function. Lined up for takeoff, the plane hesitated for a few moments, drifting slowly. People lining the shore stood quietly, anticipating the moment the plane would reach skyward. They waited, and waited some more, as the big plane sat, engines idling.

Suddenly the four engines roared to life, and the plane surged forward. The people watching craned their necks and stood on tiptoes to better their view, then all they could see was water engulfing the hull with only the wings visible. Out of this wall of water, the plane gracefully soared into the sky. The crowd broke into applause, cheering and waving at the departing aviators.

Inside the plane, Captain Williams worked the control wheel and the rudder pedals, guiding the plane accurately to achieve its best climb and keep it on course. Jack called out airspeed and altitude, ready to assist on the controls at the captain's request. Ed Butz diligently scrutinized the gauges, monitoring the life of each engine, making small adjustments. At this point the other two crew members were along for the ride, but soon their skills would be put to use.

"Mister Smith, what do you think of a flyover?" the captain asked.

"I think the people would enjoy it."

Captain Williams turned the plane in a graceful arc back toward the city and, a thousand feet above the ground, flew over houses and businesses. He then turned toward the Caribbean Airways dock, and lowering the altitude to a hundred feet, flew over the channel to the thrill of the crowd. They cheered and waved as the plane streaked past then flew off toward the south. It gradually became a dot in the sky and then vanished from sight. The people made their way back to normal morning routines.

Once established in cruise, the men dropped formalities and began to chat.

Jack had gotten to know the captain well during the past month on the scheduled run from Nassau to Havana to Miami back to Nassau. The Sikorsky S-38 they used for that route was a twin-engine amphibious plane that required only a two-person crew. Though a firm, no nonsense man who expected his pilots to perform professionally, Captain Williams relaxed once off duty, and Jack got to see his personal side.

Jack turned to the captain and, wanting the conversation to remain private, spoke directly rather than through the intercom. "Gail pulled me aside this morning when we were upstairs in the offices."

"She did?"

"Yes." Jack hesitated, then said, "She said she'd be thinking about me, about all of us, and she was worried. You know how Gail is, always concerned about things. Well, she said when we got back, she wanted me to take her for a ride on that motorcycle I bought from Ed."

"What did you say?"

"What could I say? I told her I would, said she'd enjoy it: it'd be fun."

"What about Sally Wong?"

"That's over." Jack related to the captain his final conversation with Sally.

The captain nodded. "I'm sorry to hear that, but Gail's a nice woman."

"Yeah, she is." A far-off look came into Jack's eyes, and he stared out at the distant horizon.

"Deep in thought?" the captain asked.

"Huh? Oh, yeah, I guess I am."

Lyle Ellison, who'd arrived just the day before, sat at the temporary navigator's station in the forward cabin. A table had been installed as well as a drift meter, altimeter, and airspeed indicator. A clear dome also had been added to the ceiling from which he could take sextant readings. He could communicate with the rest of the crew up on the flight deck through headphones and a microphone plugged into the intercom system. In addition, the new direction-finding radio had been installed, though Lyle had expressed his doubts about this new piece of technology. He had some experience with the Adcock system but was aware of its limited range, thus he doubted its usefulness over some of the long distances they'd be covering. Despite assurances by Harold, he didn't trust invisible radio waves and insisted that the tried-and-true navigation methods would prove more accurate.

Lyle was six feet tall and slender with medium-brown hair parted on his right side. He wore it a bit longer than was the norm, the top combed diagonally back and held in place with pomade, which gave it a wet, shiny look. He had a straight nose and a firm set to his mouth, and he smoked cigarettes, Camels, his fingertips nicotine stained. Like the rest of the crew, he wore a Caribbean Airways uniform. Though not a revenue flight, Captain Williams expected all flight crews to be in uniform at all times while flying.

"Remember that fella on our last flight to Havana?" Jack asked the captain. "The one with the scar on the left side of his face. A German name, if I recall."

"Yeah, I remember the fella."

"Holtz; that was his name. Alfred Holtz. Suppose he's connected with Colombia and South American Airways? He didn't fit the image of a typical businessman, and he certainly wasn't a tourist."

CSAA primarily flew within Colombia, though it

did offer service to areas in the interior of Venezuela, landing on lakes and rivers. The airline was based in Barranquilla, Colombia, operating from the mouth of the Magdalena River. They flew German-built Junkers W-34 float planes, and Ford AT-5C Trimotors, also on floats. Both planes were constructed of corrugated metal, but that's where the similarities ended. The Junkers plane was a low-wing single-engine and held five passengers. The Ford was high wing, had three engines, and held seventeen passengers.

The men were on course for Maracaibo, Venezuela, with a refueling stop in Kingston, Jamaica. At Maracaibo, Caribbean Airways had occasional problems with Colombia and South America Airways encroaching on their territory. CSAA even landed in the harbor at Maracaibo under the pretext of mechanical issues, though everyone knew it was to spy on the facilities. Also, though not allowed to operate in Panama, CSAA planes overflew the country and periodically flew relatively low over the canal where the American Army Air Corps pursuit planes at France Field chased them off. They were always ready to scramble at a moment's notice. Keystone bombers also stood by at the airfield to bomb hostile ships or ground forces headed to the canal.

"Think Colombia Air will cause any trouble?" Jack asked.

"Hard to say, but we need to be on guard."

"What about McClelland? I think I'd be more concerned about him. After all, the old man did pretty much ruin him."

"I guess he did, or at least hurried it along," the captain replied. "McClelland was having financial trouble, from what I understand. Don't think he was that good a businessman. But, yeah, the old man took advantage."

"Where'd he go, anyway?"

"I don't know for sure. All I've heard are a few rumors. Heard he went into gold mining somewhere deep in South America."

"If that's true, then he's in the area we're going to."

"Possibly, but South America is a big continent."

Late in the day, Lago de Maracaibo came into view, the destination for the day. The oil rigs built in the eastern side of the lake were clearly visible, tall towers of steel girders, black against the sky, that held the pumping mechanism that pulled the oil from the expansive deposits beneath the lake. A couple of tankers passed out of the lake and into the ocean, carrying the oil to refineries, and small boats scurried about, shuttling men and supplies to the rigs. Slips that held yachts registered with the International Star Class Yacht Racing Association sat along the western shore. The social clubs of the various oil companies that had a presence in Venezuela provided them as part of their recreation offerings. A couple of the yachts were gliding along the water as the plane approached. The men landed in the lake and secured the plane at the new dock built to accommodate the big plane. A Consolidated Commodore, a twin-engine seaplane that flew the Caribbean Airways scheduled route, rested at the smaller dock. The Commodore was a twenty-two passenger, 100 mph airplane that featured panoramic windows, providing passengers with a wide-open view of the world below.

The crew, suitcases in hand, walked up the dock and into the terminal where they planned to call a cab for the Hotel Hispania, a four-story stone structure with domed turrets on the corners. They met up with the pilots of the Commodore, Captain Joe Anders and copilot Roy Talbot.

The captain introduced Harold and Lyle, then asked Joe, "Running a little late tonight?"

"A little. We had some weather over Panama we had to skirt around."

"Some weather?" Roy said. "More like a storm, a big storm. It was pretty intense there for a bit. I began to wonder if we'd make it. One of the worst I've been through. Of course, Joe and I got through it, but it was intense."

"Aw, Roy, it wasn't that bad." Joe gave the captain

a slight eye-roll, which the captain acknowledged.

"We did see a strange airplane," Roy said. "Some little single-engine machine with some kinda funny markings on it. It wasn't the Junkers that Colombian has; it was somethin' different. Seemed like it was followin' us for a way, then it just disappeared."

Joe nodded. "Now that's true. I've never seen the plane before, and I didn't recognize the markings. It was a land plane too, not a float plane. Last we saw of it, it was headed toward Barranquilla. Suppose it could have belonged to Colombia Air, but it wasn't big enough to haul passengers. Suppose Colombia is using it to spy on us?"

The captain frowned. "Very well could be; we'll keep an eye out for it."

The cab for the two Commodore pilots pulled up and the men departed for the hotel. Soon the cab for the five Sikorsky crewmen arrived, and they also headed for an evening's rest.

Next day, just a few minutes before arriving at Georgetown, British Guiana, for fuel, Lyle called over the intercom, "Plane, three o'clock low."

Jack turned to see a single-engine airplane flying on a parallel path, slightly lower and about half a mile distant. The plane drifted closer.

Lyle looked through binoculars. "Yeah, single-engine, low-wing. Some kinda symbol on the tail."

On the flight deck, Jack also looked through binoculars. "Captain, looks like a swastika on the tail. Black against a red background."

"I think that's German," the captain said.

Harold got out of his seat and kneeled behind Jack. "It is. It's the Nazi symbol."

Jack followed the plane with the glasses. "Might be working with Colombia Air."

The captain reached out a hand. "Let me have a look."

Jack handed him the binoculars and took the flight controls.

The captain got up and, after Harold made room, knelt behind Jack. "Looks like a Messerschmitt 108. Four-seat plane, retractable gear, fairly quick."

The plane drifted closer again, then suddenly disappeared beneath the Sikorsky and popped up on the port side just beyond the wingtip.

Ed turned to take a look. "Two men in the plane."

The plane and the two mysterious men zoomed upward and away.

Harold frowned. "What do you suppose they're up to?"

"I don't know," Captain Williams replied, "but they were looking us over good."

"Think they're dangerous?" Jack asked.

Harold snorted. "If they're Nazis, of course they

are."

The men landed in the mouth of the Demerara River at Georgetown, the final stop on the current Caribbean Airways route. They took on fuel and made a quick inspection of the plane, then flew off to Belém, Brazil, the first port on the extension of the route into South America.

Brazil boasted of having one of the early aviators, Alberto Santos-Dumont, though he lived in Europe at the time of his venture into aviation. "The Flying Brazilian" was a sensation in Paris with his dirigible, then later his airplane, which was the first heavier-than-air machine to fly in Europe. Despite Santos-Dumont's achievements, Brazil depended on aviation technology from Europe. Germany was willing to provide that technology. In 1930, Germany's LZ127 Graf Zeppelin landed in Recife, Brazil, and it had made subsequent trips to the South American continent since.

After the Nazi party won major elections a year later, German interest in the Western Hemisphere intensified, and several groups adhering to the ideals of the Nazi party formed in Brazil. Hitler's appointment as chancellor in 1933 empowered the Brazilian groups. Along with the Nazi presence in Colombia, the party worked to expand its influence across the continent, and aviation was one of the keys to this expansion. The airplane provided access to the remote regions and quickly covered the vast distances across South America for the movement of people, equipment, and political ideas.

After following the coast from Georgetown, when over Cayenne, French Guiana, they turned southeastward for a straight-line path to Belém. As they flew over the dense, endless jungle with no distinguishing landmarks to provide reference, Harold guided Lyle in the use of the navigation radio. Harold had a nav radio installed at his own station in addition to the one for the navigator. Though a navigator wouldn't be used on the scheduled South American routes, the radio operator would use the navigation radio to help keep the pilots on track. In the future for flights across the Atlantic, and eventually the Pacific, a navigator would be part of the crew as radio navigation was the only accurate means to guide a plane over the vast expanse of water.

Radio navigation in the United States had progressed, sometimes slowly, from the early days of airmail flying when a system of lighted beacons across the country guided the pilots at night, and the names of towns and arrows pointing to the next town painted on rooftops gave daytime guidance. The drawback to this system was its uselessness in bad weather—the ground had to be visible. The next step was radio communication. By 1934, there were at least fifty radio stations for ground-to-air communication that allowed pilots to request navigation help. In addition to voice communication, the Federal Bureau of Standards had developed a radio navigation system. In 1929, the Aeronautics Branch of the Bureau made standard a four-course radio range system—pilots listened to Morse code signals to stay on course. Navigation was a little further behind in South America, but Caribbean Airways was working to change that and had installed Adcock stations along its new route, the first one in Belém.

The system the airline currently used in the Caribbean islands utilized a ground-based direction finder that received a signal from a transmitter onboard the airplane. At the ground station, the operator turned a large, rotating loop antenna, the signal becoming stronger or weaker as the antenna rotated. When the loop aligned with the airplane, they could determine the direction from the station. The ground operator then contacted the plane and provided course corrections. With the Adcock system, the aircrew determined the position from the station and guided the plane accordingly.

Four 154-foot-tall towers comprised the system, each tower at a cardinal point of the compass— north, south, east, west—plus a fifth middle tower for communication. The signal was received onboard the plane, and the pilot flew to the signal. The system did suffer from interference during thunderstorms, and the radio waves couldn't go beyond the horizon, thus limiting its effectiveness. Harold had helped correct the latter problem by using high-frequency waves that bounced off the bottom of the ionosphere, thus allowing them to follow the curvature of the earth. This long-range guidance system was waiting for aircraft capable of traversing the vast distances across the oceans. When that happened, the world would truly be connected by air.

"I don't need a radio to guide me," Lyle insisted as Harold attempted to tutor him in the use of the equipment. "Hell, look out the window and see where we are. Even if we can't see, all we need to do is follow the compass."

"All I see is endless jungle," Harold said. "What about wind drift?"

"See this gadget?" Lyle pointed to an optical sight atop an instrument that protruded from the belly of the plane. "It's a drift meter, shows me how much we're drifting off course. All I got to do is figure the drift into course calculations, and it gives me our heading."

"What if there's clouds below us?" asked Harold.

There was no response.

Lyle wasn't an aviator but a navigator, having learned his craft on ships—he held a Master Navigator's rating that allowed him to navigate to any seaport in the world. He'd done well with aerial navigation, but planes were getting faster and distances longer, and radio navigation was proving to be the best means for course guidance. But unconvinced that invisible electronic beams could really provide accurate direction, he used his time-honored and well-honed skills of manual navigation. With the drift meter, he determined wind speed and direction and used this information to calculate groundspeed and heading. He used plotter, protractor, and divider to plot the course, leaning over the charts spread out on his table in the passenger cabin. After shooting the sun with the sextant to verify position, he made any corrections necessary. Navigating had been done that way for at least a hundred years, and as far as he was concerned, it'd be used for a hundred more.

"All right, turn on the radio," Harold ordered, "and I'll show you how to tune it in to the station at Belém."

Lyle grumbled.

The radio hummed as electricity flowed through the wires and circuits, and the tubes inside the black box warmed up, their orange glow growing brighter then turning white as the heat built. Harold, puffing on his pipe, guided Lyle as he reluctantly and grudgingly twisted and turned knobs, but all that came through was the crackling and popping of static.

Harold scratched his head. "Huh."

"What's wrong?" Lyle asked. "That fancy radio not working? Guess we'll do things the right way." He turned to his charts, and Harold went back to his station on the flight deck.

"Captain, I'm not receiving any signal from Belém," Harold said. "We should have contact with the Adcock station, but I'm getting nothing."

"The radio at Belém is supposed to be in operation," said the captain.

"We don't need it," Lyle said through the intercom. "I'll get us to Belém, right dead-on to the harbor."

A couple of hours later, the Amazon River delta came into view, a wide expanse of muddy water that fanned out into the ocean. At this point they were only a little more than an hour away from Belém, where they'd land in the inlet of the Para River.

"I told you I could get us there," Lyle bragged. "I don't need your fancy radio beams."

Jack flew on the approach to Belém while Captain Williams searched for a landing lane marked by buoys. But they never appeared.

Jack frowned. "What do you think, Captain?"

"Let's circle some more. Maybe we missed seeing something."

Harold made contact with the maritime radio station and asked for landing and docking instructions.

"Radio, got any instructions from the maritime station?" the captain asked.

"The man said to land anywhere," Harold replied. "Just don't hit anything."

"What? They're supposed to have a dock for us and a landing area marked out. And nothing from the Adcock. What's going on?"

"Don't know, Captain. The fella wouldn't say much, just land anywhere."

"Jack, take it on down for a closer look at the harbor."

Jack guided the plane low over the harbor, all eyes of the crew searching for an open spot to land. They flew down the length of the river that widened as it approached the ocean and provided a generous area for boat traffic and docking.

"Looks like a good open area just below and to port," the captain said. "Turn around and go straight out a couple of miles, then come back for landing."

The big plane touched down in a spray of water and slowed, engines idling, as it taxied toward the docks. The sun was sinking fast.

"Captain, we can't get up to the docks. Shall we anchor out here?" Jack said.

"Yes, it's all we can do."

Ed scurried down into the nose of the plane where an anchor was stowed for such occasions, and upon Jack's command, he lowered it.

"Harold," asked the captain, "any word on a boat to pick us up?"

"I told them to send one. I'll call again."

Finally, out of the encroaching darkness, a small boat slowly chugged toward them. Captain Williams threw open the hatch and waved to the boater, who then bumped alongside and stopped.

"Need a ride?" a skinny man with a dark, bushy mustache asked in clear English. He wore a red kerchief about his neck and a battered whoopee hat—a fedora with the brim cut in scallops and turned up.

"Yes. There's five of us, and we have some luggage."

"It's all right. You can fit."

"That boat seems kind of small for all of us."

"No worry. Climb aboard."

"Give us a couple of moments to gather our belongings, and we'll be there."

The man settled back in his boat, patiently waiting.

The five men boarded the boat, each one dragging

a small suitcase. The boat sat lower in the water as each man stepped aboard.

"All right, we're set," the captain said.

"Here we go." The boat operator pushed away from alongside the airplane and started the small engine.

The boat filled with men slowly chugged toward the dock. The engine putted along uncertainly with the water dangerously close to the gunwales.

"This place stinks!" Harold exclaimed as they neared the shore.

The man guiding the boat said, "It's distilled wood."

"Smells like sewage to me!"

Once at the dock, Captain Williams inquired about a hotel, and the man directed them to accommodations within walking distance. Once there, the men faced a building that didn't look the least bit luxurious. The stucco crumbled, faded green shutters hung crookedly on rusted hinges, and the green awning above the front entrance was ripped. Since they had to pay out of their own pockets, they bunked three in one room and two in another room to save money. The hotel clerk wouldn't accept credit from Caribbean Airways and insisted on money in his hand before he showed the men to their rooms. Captain Williams demanded a receipt, which the clerk, a small, mousy fella with a thin mustache, grudgingly provided.

Once in their rooms, the men gathered in Captain Williams and Jack's room for a conference. "What's going on here?" Jack asked. "No welcoming committee. No arrangements. It's like they didn't even expect us."

The captain shrugged. "I don't know."

"Let's find a place to eat," said Harold. "I'm getting hungry and feeling a little weak."

The men found a dingy hole-in-the-wall café just down the street. As they ate, they discussed the situation.

"How much fuel do we have?" the captain asked of Ed.

"About two hours, and that's without reserves."

"If we can't get fuel here, we'll have to arrange for some within 150 miles, 200 at the most. And what are the odds of finding aviation fuel?"

"What if we can't get any?" Harold asked. "We'll be stuck in this dreadful place for who knows how long."

Ed snorted. "Aw, don't get excited. We'll get fuel. Somehow."

When the men returned to the hotel, just as they got to the top of the stairs to the second floor where their rooms were located, a door slammed, and footsteps echoed down the wooden rear stairs.

"Who was that?" Jack asked.

"He just left our room!" Lyle yelled.

Ed turned and ran down the front stairs, hoping to catch the man if he came around the front of the building. For a short, somewhat stocky man, he was quick as lightning and disappeared before the others knew what happened. Jack ran down the back stairs, followed by Captain Williams, while Harold and Lyle remained guarding the room. They threw on the light switch to find open suitcases and clothes tossed about the room.

"Did he get anything?" Harold asked in a panic, nearly dropping the pipe from his mouth, as he knelt to retrieve shirts, socks, and shorts.

Lyle shrugged. "Check and see."

Two of the three suitcases had been tampered with, but the men determined that nothing was taken.

Shortly Jack and the captain returned, having lost the unknown man.

"Who do you suppose he was?" Harold asked.

"Maybe from Colombia and South American Airways," Jack said.

Lyle put a fresh Camel to his lips. "Maybe. Or a local fellow hired to do a job."

"A robber?" Harold suggested.

Lyle shook his head. "I don't think so. He knew

what room to get into. He's probably looking for navigation charts, looking for our route, see what we're up to."

The captain nodded. "I think you're right. Maybe our German friends."

"Think so?" Harold asked.

"The odds are good," the captain replied, "so we need to be on our guard."

Lyle looked around. "Say, where'd Butz go?"

"I wouldn't worry about him," the captain said. "He'll find his way back."

At breakfast in the drab café the next morning, Ed said, "Wasn't able to catch that fella last night, but I've got fuel lined up. A boat will meet us in an hour. We have to pay the man directly. We have enough money?"

"How much fuel we need?" the captain asked.

"Enough for the flight to Sao Luis. That will give us plenty of reserve with the two hours left in the tanks. We do have fuel and facilities confirmed there, don't we?"

The captain nodded. "We do. I called last night to confirm, and everything's in order."

"Get a deal on the price?" Jack asked.

"Yeah, but it's still kinda steep. Forty-two cents a gallon. That's US gallons, I made sure of that."

The captain's eyebrows rose. "That is a bit steep.

How much was he asking?"

"Fifty cents."

"I'll call New York," the captain said, "have them wire down the money."

Ed continued, "Also, we're supposed to meet with some officials today. They'll seek us out at the hotel. I did get a line on that prowler. He's most likely a German—probably a Nazi—at least, that's the consensus."

Lyle nodded. "Just what I thought. He was looking for information."

"The man in that small plane? You know, the one with the Nazi symbol on the tail?" Harold asked.

Jack nodded. "Most likely."

Harold sighed. "So what are we going to do? What if the fella keeps following us?"

Ed said, "He most likely will. We just have to keep our eyes open."

The captain pushed aside his empty plate. "We better get going. We have a lot to do."

"It's going to take all morning to get things done," Jack said. "How much flying time will we need to get to Fortaleza?"

"Five hours," Lyle said. "We get out of here by noon, we'll be in good shape."

Harold relit his pipe. "Unless we get hung up in Sao Luis. Which I don't doubt. We may have to do some meet-and-greet stuff with the local officials. Who knows what they have planned for us."

"If we can wrap it up there by four o'clock, we'll get to Fortaleza just before dark," said the captain. "We can't get away in time, we'll spend the night."

The men finished breakfast and returned to the hotel. Captain Williams called from the lobby phone to arrange for money transfer. The men gathered up their belongings and met in the lobby in anticipation of meeting the city officials. Soon a couple of men wearing white suits and wide-brimmed white hats appeared, one stout-built, the other man tall and skinny.

The stout man breathed heavily and wiped sweat from his brow. "The men from the airplane, I presume?"

"Yes sir," replied the captain.

"We're sorry we weren't here last night to meet you," the skinny man said.

"Yes, we are sorry," said the other man. "Are you finding everything satisfactory?"

"No, we're not," the captain replied bluntly. "No docking facilities, overpriced fuel which our man here had to scrounge for, poor accommodations, and the Adcock wasn't working. We also had an intruder last night."

The stout man's eyes widened. "Oh? An intruder?"

"Yes, someone looking for information, I'm sure."

"Not just a robber?"

"I don't think so. Nothing was missing."

"Are you sure?"

The usually calm captain gave a terse reply, "I think we'd know if we had personal effects missing."

"Yes, I guess you would."

The group of men took seats in the lobby in order to continue the discussion. The Caribbean Air crew posed direct questions that made the two officials from the City of Belém sweat and squirm. The meeting ended with handshakes and promises for facilities in place by the time scheduled services began.

As the men waited for the refueling boat and the small boat to take them to the plane, they discussed their experience.

"I think those two fellas knew exactly who that was that broke into our room," Jack said. "That's the reason we never saw them until this morning; they wanted to stay clear so we wouldn't suspect them."

"I wonder if they're really with the city," said Harold, pipe in hand.

Ed nodded. "I wondered that too."

The boat with the fuel pulled up to the dock, and Ed boarded to supervise refueling and pay the man. Shortly another boat appeared and took the rest of the men to the anchored plane. The crew performed a thorough preflight check and then flew to Sao Luis, which proved to be an uneventful flight. As Harold predicted, city officials met them, and a crowd lined the waterfront, cheering and waving. It all went smoothly, and they touched down in Fortaleza just after seven in the evening. Officials met them at the dock and took them to a first-class hotel, in stark contrast to the previous night's accommodations.

After an evening meal, the men, now out of flight uniforms, wandered out into the hot, humid night. People filled the streets, the men in light-colored trousers and shirts and the women in long, flowing dresses. Street musicians tuned up instruments, the smells of food lingered in the air, and voices rose and fell as groups of people strolled along. A group of musicians began playing *baiao*, a traditional music of the region. The music had a syncopated beat with a driving bass drum and fills on a triangle beneath the sound of guitars. The men watched and listened, and soon dancers began to sway to the rhythms. From there the men moved on down the street and sampled *baiao de dois*, a food named for the music, which consisted of black-eyed peas and rice.

The group of five men became a group of three when Ed and Lyle both disappeared, each in different directions. Unknown to them another Caucasian drifted in and out among the crowds, a bareheaded man with light-colored hair combed straight back, a scar on his left cheek, and wearing horn-rimmed glasses. The mysterious fellow watched the Caribbean Airways men and kept track of their movement, always in the shadows or blended into a crowd. He followed them until they returned to the hotel.

Hungry Jungle

After being awake for over fifty hours, the green of the endless canopy of rainforest trees became a blur, with no north, south, east, or west, just green below and blue sky above. The fuel gauges bounced off their empty marks, the single engine seemingly running on fumes before it sputtered to a stop.

Down in the jungle, Paul Redfern, twenty-five years old, confident and with a swagger about him, was unaware if it was reality or just a dream; his mind was so dazed and numbed from sleep deprivation.

Inspired by Lindbergh's solo flight, he wanted to prove himself and best the distance record by flying forty-six hundred miles from Brunswick, Georgia, to Rio de Janeiro, making the trip nonstop, alone. After fifty hours without sleep, crossing the glistening blue Caribbean, then over the endless green jungle of the South American continent, fatigue distorted his perception, and reality blended into grayness.

Engine out of fuel, the plane flew silent now. The blue sky and green jungle swirled together as the plane skimmed the jungle canopy. Then came the crunching sounds of crumpling metal. The treetops opened as the plane slid through, then closed behind it, as if it had been eaten and swallowed, leaving it invisible to anyone searching from overhead. The young pilot, uninjured but sleep deprived, dozed off. He awoke in the middle of the night to find the chirp of bugs and howling of monkeys had replaced the sound of the droning engine.

Since that August in 1927, rumors still abounded that he was alive somewhere deep within the rainforest, living with a native tribe. Even in 1934, his family still clung to that hope.

Chapter Five

Next morning at breakfast in the hotel café, Lyle showed up as the other four men were finishing.

"Lyle, you look terrible," Ed said.

"Thanks, Butz, that sure makes me feel better."

"On a bender last night?"

"No, just had a few drinks." With unsteady hands, he lit a cigarette.

Captain Williams regarded him with concern. "You be ready to go in one hour."

"Don't concern yourself about me; I'll be ready."

Harold packed his pipe, silently taking it all in.

"Well, Ed, what did you do last night?" Jack asked. "Get anything good?"

He nodded. "Got something real good. Found out who that fella might be who broke into our room back in Belém. A German named Alfred Holtz."

Jack's eyebrows rose. "That's the same fella that was on our Havana flight. I knew there was something about him!"

"Yeah, a spy, a Nazi spy. Supposedly got into a mess in Guatemala. Rumor has it, he killed a fella."

"Who's he working for?" the captain asked. "The German government or Colombia and South American Air?"

"Not sure if he's directly connected with the airline. But he does have a plane, a single-engine machine."

"The one we saw?" Jack asked.

"Yeah, a Messerschmitt 108. It's a land plane, so he's a bit restricted where he can land, but there are a few strips hacked out of the jungle."

"So what's a Messerschmitt 108 used for?" Jack asked. "It can't haul much of a load."

"They were built for the Challenge in Poland held this spring," the captain explained. "It's for touring aircraft and intended to promote flying in Europe. It's a nimble plane, pretty quick, and can take off and land in a relatively short distance. Just the thing for getting around over here."

"So Holtz, if he's flying it, can easily follow us."

The captain nodded. "Very easily."

Lyle ordered toast and coffee and took a couple

of aspirin, and by the time the men were ready to go to the plane, he at least gave the appearance of being human.

The morning was clear and the wind light, a perfect start to the flight to Recife, a relatively short trip of about 550 miles. They should cover that distance in about three and a half hours, then they'd go on to Salvador.

The flight went smoothly at first, and the men relaxed, confident in the plane and in themselves, until Ed called, "Losing power on number four."

The men snapped to attention. Beneath them was only jungle, a solid canopy of treetops; no open spot in which to land. Even if they found an open area, it'd do them no good because the plane's boat-like hull would crumple on touchdown. The ocean was many miles distant.

"What's going on?" Harold asked, his voice going up an octave.

"Nothin' you need to worry about," Ed said.

"Keep an eye on it," the captain said calmly. "Any ideas?"

"Not yet. Fuel is on and fuel pressure's good. Oil pressure and temp are good. I'll try the mixture."

"Do what you can."

Jack glanced at the captain. "What'll we do if we lose the engine?"

"At this point, we'll continue on to Recife. We'll fly just fine on three."

"Are we all right?" Harold asked. "We're in trouble, aren't we? One of the engines is sounding strange. I know it is!"

"Radio, focus on your job!" the captain commanded.

"Yes sir."

"I can feel an engine slowing down," Jack said in his slow Missouri drawl.

"Mechanic," Captain Williams called. "Give an update."

"We're definitely losing number four. I've tried everything. Acts like it's runnin' outta fuel. Could be the carburetor. Gauges show we have fuel going to the engine, but it doesn't seem to be gettin' in the cylinders. Be ready to secure the engine."

Ed would cut the fuel mixture and switch off the magnetos, and the pilots would feather the propeller. A feathered prop was one with the blades turned parallel to the airflow in order to reduce drag and prevent windmilling of the dead engine.

The engine lost power quickly and began to shudder and backfire. It was time to put it out of its misery.

The big propeller jerked to a stop as the engine breathed its last, leaving the work of pulling the plane through the air to the other three engines. Speed and altitude decreased slightly. Had there been passengers aboard, they most likely wouldn't have realized an engine had been shut down. As long as the other three remained healthy, the flight would face no jeopardy.

"What are we gonna do?" Harold sounded nervous.

"We're going to fly," Captain Williams replied.

"But for how long?"

"As long as we need to."

The men flew on, though idle chatter died. Each man concentrated on his job, the dead propeller a reminder that things weren't normal.

Then engine number three backfired and jerked to a stop.

Harold screamed, "What's happening?"

"Lost number three!" Ed said. "Captain, feather the prop; I'll kill the mags."

"Roger."

The two powerful engines and big propellers on the port wing yawed and rolled the plane to the right, threatening to send it out of control and spiraling into the dense jungle below. Harold grabbed the edge of his table as the flight deck tilted and the plane began its fall. Lyle grabbed for his charts, pencils, and plotters as they started to slide off his table. But Ed monitored gauges as usual—this was no different for him than spinning in a Sopwith Camel.

As the green of the jungle filled the windscreen, both pilots stood on their left rudder pedals, pushing with all the strength their legs could muster, and turned their control wheels left. The captain reached overhead for the throttles and eased back on the power on the two good engines to reduce the adverse yaw. Once again, blue sky above, green below, filled the view outside the flight deck. The plane returned to level flight, and the men started breathing again. Still, the flight would require left rudder pressure and a bit of left aileron for the entire distance. The pilots would have sore left legs next morning.

"Butz, what's going on?" asked the captain.

"Don't know for sure. This one didn't give any warning at all, runnin' just fine 'til it backfired and quit. It's like the fuel just shut off."

Jack frowned. "Carburetors?"

"Could be; but for them both to malfunction?"

The plane now limped along, slower and a little lower, as the men figured a course of action. They couldn't afford to lose another engine. The jungle appeared tranquil from the air, a carpet of green trees growing densely together and going on as far as the eye could see. But it seemed to reach up for them, ready to pluck them out of the air.

"Lyle, set a course for the coast," the captain said.

Though the plane was following the radio

navigation signal to Recife—Lyle had reluctantly given in to the new technology—this was his chance to demonstrate his trusted navigating system.

"Roger, but there's a lake about forty miles ahead, half the distance. Only need to deviate a few degrees."

"Big enough to land on?"

"Plenty big."

"Roger."

"Gonna try for the lake?" Jack asked.

"Yeah, it's a lot closer."

"Look." Jack pointed to the two o'clock position. "Clouds. Low with some heavy rain."

The men now faced a serious situation—forge ahead for the lake or turn toward the coast for assurances of landing. If they lost another engine on the way to the coast, their odds would be slim of making it. One-engine performance was virtually nonexistent, and the jungle would claim them, maybe permanently. If they remained on course and raced the clouds to the lake, they could lose the race, arriving at the lake just as visibility reached zero.

After studying the clouds, Captain Williams elected to continue on.

The lake came into view over the nose, and the plane began to descend for landing. There would be only one chance. They couldn't get too low because the plane had little climb ability left, so the pilots had to judge accurately to establish the correct glide path. They decided to remain a little high because they could always lose altitude by adding more flaps or putting the plane into a slip to create drag along the side of the fuselage.

Harold and Lyle had become passengers at this point, but the two pilots worked together to control the plane, and Ed closely monitored functions on the remaining engines. As they began final approach, rain began to fall and the wind gusted violently. A gust lifted them, putting them above their approach path. They had to descend quickly.

"Reduce power!" Captain Williams called.

Jack reached overhead and pulled the throttles back on the two remaining engines. "Full flaps," he called as he pushed forward on the control wheel to get the nose down to descend. But he had to be careful not to get too nose-down so close to the water. If the wind suddenly quit, they would plunge nose first. If they needed to add power, it had to be done carefully because a sudden burst of asymmetric power could send them out of control and cartwheeling into the water.

The rain came down harder, beginning to pound the windscreen, which reduced visibility even more at this critical point just feet above the water. The pounding of the rain on the aluminum fuselage was deafening. Lightning flashed. The pilots pulled back on the control wheels, both of them working together to raise the nose for landing. The plane hit the water and a shudder ran through the length of the fuselage. Not a pretty landing, but they were down in one piece. The wind blew even harder as the plane came to a stop, so Ed scrambled into the bow to lower the anchor so they wouldn't be blown all over the lake. The rain pounded so hard that the men could hardly hear themselves talk, even through the aid of the intercom. They kept the two good engines idling to produce electrical power.

After the storm blew over, the men helped Ed inspect the engines. He pulled the carburetor off number four engine, took it into the cabin, and carefully disassembled it, meticulously checking each part for any defects.

"Huh!" he exclaimed.

"What'd you find, Butz?" asked the captain, who assisted him.

"Fuel inlet screen's plugged. That's the only thing I can find wrong."

"Plugged! With what?"

"That's a bit of a mystery. It looks like mud."

"Mud?"

"Looks like."

"Could it be contaminants from the fuel? That

load we got in Fortaleza may have been polluted."

"That was a supply from our own facilities, and I sampled it good."

"I know you did. But somehow it didn't show in the samples?"

"You know, it's awfully thick, like it was packed into the screen. I don't think it was from contaminants."

"Sabotage?"

"Maybe. It's a possibility. Be interesting to see if number three has the same problem. We better check the carburetors on the port engines, too."

"Can you clean those screens good enough to get us out of here?" the captain asked.

"Easy enough. I've got some solvent stored with the tools and supplies in the back. I'll get this carburetor put back together. The others don't need to be removed. Just pull the fuel line, and I can pull out the screens and clean them. Not a big job."

All the men worked, under Ed's direction, opening inspection panels on the engine cowlings and removing fuel inlet lines so he could inspect the screens. The men stood on the work platforms that lowered from the leading edges of the wings, eight platforms, each engine with one on a side. They removed coats and ties, but still they sweated in the tropical heat and humidity. The sweat ran down their faces and into their eyes. Each man had smudges on his face from wiping away the sweat with dirty hands.

Their estimated arrival time at Recife passed, and Harold tried to contact the maritime station to let them know what had happened. But at ground level, the radio wouldn't transmit far enough, and all he could hear was the crack and pop of static. The men were on their own.

The sound of an approaching plane pulled them from their work. They gazed upward, searching for the source of the sound, hands shading their eyes. The sound droned closer, then became more distinct—a single-engine airplane. It flew a couple of thousand feet overhead, turned back, lower this time, and circled the downed men twice before it faded off into the distance.

Jack shook his head. "Looks like our German friends."

"Huh!" Harold scratched his head. "Wonder how they found us."

"Obviously, they know our exact route." Ed chomped down on a fresh cigar. "They gotta be getting the information somehow."

"But how?" Harold asked.

Ed shrugged. "They've maybe got a contact somewhere."

The men found the fuel screens on engines one

and two to be free of contamination, but number three was packed with the same mysterious substance as on number four. As the men worked, Jack asked Ed, "Would it be easy for someone to have sabotaged the engines?"

"Yeah, relatively easy. From the dock, they could've climbed up to the top of the fuselage and out onto the wings. Then all they'd have to do is remove an inspection panel, pull a fuel line and smear it with this stuff, then reconnect it."

"We ought to post a guard with the plane from now on," Jack suggested.

By the time the maintenance work was done, it was getting late in the day, but if all went well they could make it to Recife just before dark.

~

Don Wilcox paced the communications room while Gail, Vivian, and Roger Brown—temporary head of maintenance in Ed's absence—watched on. "We haven't heard from them all day. They left on time this morning in Fortaleza, and they should have been in Recife a couple of hours ago. But Recife hasn't heard from them." He snuffed out a cigarette butt in an ashtray on the tabletop, pulled another cigarette from the pocket of his rumpled white shirt, and lit it.

"I'll need to call the old man, let him know what's happening."

Gail turned her back to the others and began to cry.

Vivian turned to Gail and said softly, "They're all right. I just know they are."

"How can you be so sure?" she sobbed.

"I just know. They're highly qualified, all of them."

"But things can still happen."

"We don't know that anything happened. They're just a couple of hours behind schedule."

Gail dabbed her eyes with a handkerchief. "You better be right."

"I know I am."

Wilcox and Roger discussed mechanical issues, anything that could go wrong: engine failure, flight-control malfunction, structural damage. Then they looked at weather reports and noted the intense storm that had crossed the plane's flight path. But the pilots of Caribbean Airways were quite familiar with tropical thunderstorms and gave them the respect they deserved. Still, a storm could delay them.

The radio crackled. "Nassau radio, Caribbean Air flight three-two, over."

"I'll get it, Gail." Vivian swung the swivel chair around, picked up the microphone, and responded, "Go ahead Caribbean Air."

While Vivian took care of communication and

Gail sniffled, the men continued their conversation.

"So what about engine failure?" Wilcox asked. "It can fly on three, can't it?"

"It can fly fine. Not quite as fast and not quite as high, but it will fly and handle fine."

"On two?"

"That depends upon several factors. Two out on the same side or opposite sides? How high is the terrain? Are the good engines putting out full power?"

"Roger, Caribbean Air," came from the radio.

"Ladies, put a call through to Recife," Wilcox ordered. "Have them call us immediately when the men arrive." He and Roger left the communications room.

"Nassau radio out." Vivian set the microphone down.

"Vivian," Gail said, "I'm so scared." Her eyes began to well up again. "Jack is with them." She paused. Vivian waited for her to continue. "I was to go for a ride with him on his motorcycle when they got back. I'm afraid I'll never see him or any of the others again." She hung her head as tears again began to roll.

~

Ed set the mixture to full rich and hit the starter

switch. The propeller on engine number four turned in lazy circles. After several revolutions, he switched on the magnetos. The propeller continued turning, but the engine remained silent. Ed stopped cranking in order to let the starter motor cool down.

"What's wrong?" Harold asked.

"Gotta get the carburetor filled with fuel," Ed said. "It may take a bit. Just hang on."

Again the big propeller made its lazy circles, then the engine coughed, and a puff of smoke shot from the exhaust pipe. Ed continued cranking, and the engine coughed, smoked again, then sputtered. The propeller jerkily increased its speed, and more smoke drifted back from the engine. Suddenly, it bellowed with a throaty roar and the propeller became a blur. Ed throttled it back.

Harold breathed a sigh of relief.

Since the carburetors hadn't been removed from the other three engines, the starting proceeded normally, and soon all four engines idled easily.

"Captain," Ed said. "We'll let it idle until the oil gets warm, and then do a thorough run-up."

"Roger."

"In the meantime, I'm going out to verify there's no fuel leaks. We don't need to risk a fire."

"Don't you want the engines shut down?" asked the captain.

"Negative. I want to check while the fuel lines are under full pressure."

"Radio," Captain Williams called. "Go assist Ed. I don't want him out there alone. Guard him so he doesn't slip."

"Yes, Captain."

Ed and Harold made their way out through the hatch, up to the top of the wing, and out toward number four engine, the prop still turning in its lazy circles. Though it turned so slowly that the blades were visible, it would kill in an instant if Ed fell into it.

"Jack," Captain Williams said, "keep close watch on Ed and Harold. If you even sense either of them slipping toward a prop, let me know immediately, and I'll kill the engine." He then slid into Ed's seat amid the valves and gauges in order to have quick access to the fuel cutoff.

"Yes sir." Jack went to the open hatch so he could get a good view of the wing and the engines.

"Lyle," the captain called. "Watch those two on the wing. Let me know immediately if it even looks like they're in trouble."

"Yes sir."

From the passenger cabin, Lyle would have a different view than Jack of the activity. Captain Williams wanted all bases covered as well as possible.

He didn't want to lose either man to an accident.

Ed pulled a length of rope from the toolbox and tied it around his waist. Harold held the other end, and Ed eased onto the extended work platform while Harold kept the rope taut. The propeller was only an arm's length away from Ed—any slip or misstep would be fatal. With a screwdriver Ed loosened an access panel on the side of the nacelle. The breeze from the prop blew his hair and whipped the collar and the sleeves of his coveralls. He squinted against the blast. Holding the access cover in one hand so it wouldn't blow away, he felt the fuel line leading into the carburetor, checking for any sign of cool liquid or even a hint of moisture. He felt along the carburetor, especially on the bottom where leaking fuel would run down. Then he pulled a flashlight from his pocket and visually checked for leaks or anything else amiss. Satisfied, he secured the access panel and climbed back atop the wing. He repeated the procedure three more times, then climbed back in through the hatch.

"Looks good, Captain," he reported.

The oil having reached operating temperature, Ed checked each engine one at a time, bringing up the RPM and checking the usual: magneto operation, carburetor heat, oil pressure, manifold pressure. Pleased, he said, "Captain, we're good."

Ed retrieved the sea anchor and as soon as he

settled back in at his station, Jack, the pilot flying, readied for takeoff. He turned the big plane into the wind, what little wind there was now the storm had passed, but each little bit helped shorten the takeoff distance. Once positioned, he gradually eased the throttles forward until the engines were at full power. The plane slowly increased speed. The spray of water from the hull rose higher and higher, and the bow rose, the plane skimming the surface.

The takeoff run took longer than normal due to the lack of a good head wind, and the lakeshore and tree-covered hills came closer and closer. The captain called out airspeeds to Jack, and when they finally reached lift-off speed, Jack eased back on the control wheel, and the plane rose from the water. He leveled off to build up speed. The hills grew closer, beginning to fill the windscreen, then with extra speed built up, he nosed up into a climb. The treetops, green and lush, skimmed by, seeming to just tickle the underside of the plane. Once at a safe altitude, Jack began to breathe again.

By the time Recife appeared over the nose, it was nearing dusk, and the shadows fell long over the city of three hundred thousand people. Downtown buildings were multistory structures of light-colored stone with turrets and domes jutting skyward, and homes lined the winding streets that angled in multiple directions directed by the three main rivers that flowed through the city. Islands, mangroves, beaches, and reefs made up the area, the name Recife alluding to the stone reefs offshore. Due to the abundance of water and small islands, the city was referred to as the "Brazilian Venice." On the streets, electric trams powered through overhead wires shuttled back and forth on tracks through the city. Known as Zeppelin trams—after the Graf Zeppelin that visited Recife in May 1930—and made of bare aluminum, they resembled Pullman railroad cars. The trams shared streets with cars, the Ford Model T and Model A being most common with a few Cadillacs and Auburns of the affluent. Amid this powered transportation, horses carrying people and pulling carts and wagons struggled to maintain their presence.

The dock for the Caribbean Airways base was situated in the harbor between Recife Island and the mainland. After overflying the harbor, Jack turned the plane back and circled around to a perfect landing, then taxied it up to the big new dock.

A well-dressed man in a dark suit met the crew at the dock. "Welcome to Recife!"

"Thank you," Captain Williams said. "The facilities here look good."

"We welcome Caribbean Airways. Your service

will greatly benefit our city. Now follow me, and I will take you to your accommodations."

Two United States Navy sailors came down the walkway, each with a rifle over his shoulder.

"The men from the navy will guard your plane," the man in the suit said.

The sailors stopped and one of them said, "Captain, we'll have a guard posted all night at the plane. Two guards per shift. You'll have nothing to worry about."

"Thank you, sir. How do you know we need guarding?"

"We have orders to keep watch over your airplane. A navy vessel is in the area and will be docking here shortly."

"Well, thank goodness," Harold said, breathing a sigh of relief.

"We suspect we were sabotaged last night in Fortaleza, so we're grateful for your help," the captain explained.

"It won't happen here, sir."

The sailors marched on down to the plane and took up their posts.

The men settled into the hotel, a stucco-covered building within walking distance of the harbor. It had a luxurious lobby and comfortable rooms of which each man had his own. A first-class restaurant adjoined the hotel. And a navy guard stood in the hallway leading to the men's rooms.

The men gathered in Captain Williams's room.

"First-class all the way," commented Lyle.

Harold nodded. "I'll say. And those navy guards reinforce my thoughts that we were sabotaged. They must know something we don't."

The captain looked thoughtful. "There's more going on here than we realize. It has to be connected with that German plane we've been seeing."

"And that Holtz character," Jack added.

"I'll see what I can find out," Ed said. "Do a little investigating tonight; see what turns up."

The captain nodded. "All right, Butz. And anyone else with any big ideas, be ready to go early in the morning. Up at daybreak, so judge accordingly for any activities this evening. And don't forget you're representing Caribbean Airways and the United States."

A knock came at the door.

The captain opened it to a man in a US Navy officer's uniform. "Yes, sir?" he said.

"Max Williams?" asked the officer.

"Yes."

"I'm Captain Mark Spencer with the naval vessel that just arrived here in Recife. May I have a word with you and your men?"

"Certainly. Come on in, Captain."

The navy captain entered the room and quietly closed the door behind him. "Good evening, gentlemen," he began. "As you know, I sent some men ahead and posted them to guard your airplane, and I have a man in the hallway here for your own protection. We've been watching the coastal area of this region of Brazil for a period of time now. We feel it may be a vital area for certain European interests who want to enter the Western Hemisphere."

Harold, who sat on a corner of the bed packing his pipe, and Lyle, who lounged in the overstuffed chair, got up, stood with the other men and edged closer to hear Captain Spencer's words.

"They may want to take advantage of the relatively short distance between western Africa and eastern South America, and that means they'd land in this region whether by boat or by airplane. As you know, the Graf Zeppelin docks in Buenos Aires already, but we think the Germans want to proceed across the continent. Winged aircraft are the most practical means for that."

"We've already encountered a German along the way," Ed said. "We're pretty certain he's tried to break into our rooms."

"We're aware of him and his accomplice."

Jack raised an eyebrow. "Accomplice?"

"We know he has at least one fella working closely with him, maybe more. We're certain they're Nazi German espionage agents. Their mission is to let you establish the air routes, facilities, and fuel supplies, but prevent you from actually flying scheduled service. And they'll prevent this by any means possible. Sabotage to the plane or even eliminating you, then their country's air service will move in to take over."

"Colombia and South American Airways?" the captain asked.

"Most likely. I'm sure you're aware that Germany has been assisting them with pilots and planes."

"We're aware."

"Where are you headed next?" Captain Spencer asked.

"Salvador, then Rio, and finally on down to Buenos Aires. But we're going to spend an extra day here going over the plane, make sure it's good for the rest of the trip."

Captain Spencer nodded. "Salvador should present no problems. I know your facilities are in place there. And when you get to Rio, contact this man." He handed Captain Williams a piece of paper with a name and phone number written on it. "He's working with us and will make sure you're safe there. He has investigated the local officials and the police department to see who can be trusted, and fortunately nearly everyone can be. He'll make sure the best men guard your plane. As for Buenos Aires, the information I have is a bit sketchy, but you need to be on your guard there. Indications are it's a center for Nazi activity."

"Thanks for the heads-up," the captain said.

"Can we leave the hotel this evening?" Lyle asked. "The guard in the hallway."

"Yes. Move about freely. The guard is only to keep unwanted people out."

Captain Spencer looked at Ed. "Be careful who you deal with down here, Mister Butz." With that word of warning imparted, he said, "Good evening, gentlemen. If you need anything, let the guard know and word will get to me." Then he turned and went out the door.

"Butz, your mouth is open," Captain Williams said.

Ed's cigar was now in his hand. "Yeah."

"Maybe you're not as secretive as you think."

"Well, those fellas got to be good to keep tabs on me."

"Heed his advice. Get in jail here, we probably can't get you out. Or worse, you may get beaten up or killed."

"I'll be careful. I gotta nose for business."

"Don't go getting that nose broken."

"Girls!" Don Wilcox burst into the communications room. "We've just got word from Recife!"

Vivian, who'd stayed past her shift awaiting word of the men, broke into a big smile, anticipating the good news, while Gail went pale, anticipating bad news, the fate of the men being almost too much for her to bear. "The men just landed there a short while ago."

Gail let out her breath and began to cry again, this time for relief and joy, rather than fear and sadness.

"Did they have a problem with the plane?" Vivian asked.

"Seems they had some engine trouble. They set down somewhere on a lake or river and got it fixed. Put them way behind schedule."

"I hope everything's working all right now," Gail said.

"As far as I know, it is. I haven't heard otherwise." He hesitated a moment in the doorway, then said, "I thought you ladies should know what's going on."

Vivian smiled. "Thank you, Mister Wilcox. We appreciate the news."

After Wilcox left, Vivian turned to Gail. "I told you the fellas were all right. I could feel it."

"I wish I had your confidence. I worry too much, I know. But when you don't hear, and the fellas are in such a remote place, you can't help but be concerned."

"I know. I do say prayers for their safety. Don't think I have no concern, but I have faith they'll be all right. And I can feel it."

Vivian paused, then said, "Mister Jack will be back just fine. I know he will."

"I know. But it's hard not to worry."

"It is. But they're experienced, and they're careful. They're not stunt fliers."

"It's just that they're so far away, and I know that some of that land they fly over is so remote. They could be there for days before anyone could find them or before they could find their way to civilization."

"Miss Gail," Vivian said, "why don't you come have an evening meal with my husband and I and the kids? We'd like to have your company."

Gail smiled. "Thank you, Vivian. I'll accept your offer. I know I shouldn't be alone all evening."

"You shouldn't. We'll see you later. I'm going home now; it's been a long day."

Vivian left, and Gail stayed to finish her shift, which wouldn't end before all planes were accounted for and resting safely at their destinations.

The rest of the evening was uneventful—the radio communications routine, the weather beautiful, the skies clear, and the air smooth. On her way out of the terminal after her shift, Gail paused and looked at the dock where a pair of S-38s rocked gently with the waves. They'd spend the night there until the crews arrived next morning to begin a new day, then they'd wing their way to destinations across the Caribbean Sea to Kingston or San Juan or Saint Thomas, or some other exotic port of call. In some of those faraway ports, planes also rested at docks, waiting for morning when they'd return to Nassau, home base where they'd receive inspection, maintenance, and cleaning for their next flight, seemingly tireless in winging their way through the tropical skies.

Radio Shows

It was time. Fingers grasped the knob and turned the radio on, then grasped the other knob and tuned in the proper station, turning slowly, precisely, hunting for the exact spot to get the strongest signal. Mother, father, and kids settled back in the living room—each in their place whether in a chair or cross-legged on the floor—and listened intently.

In addition to movies, radio, as well as delivering the news, served as an escape from reality. Radio heroes whisked listeners off to faraway, exotic locations where they engaged in high adventure, chasing pirates or bank robbers or rescuing people from dire situations.

Any place a radio could receive a signal, whether in a city or in the hills and hollers of remote rural areas, people of all walks of life came together, unknown to each other, and shared in thrills and adventures far removed from the drab, everyday existence of their lives.

These magic boxes full of wires and tubes came in cathedral and tombstone tabletop models, as well as in bigger floor models that fit into the room as a piece of furniture. No matter the make or model, these wooden designs, with matching cloth covering the single speaker, had two knobs on the front: one for volume and one for tuning in the correct station. A dial—backlit, with numbers on it and a pointer moved by the tuning knob—indicated the frequencies for the stations.

Chapter Six

The Red Garter Parlor was one in a row of hole-in-the-wall establishments that lined the dirty, narrow brick street. The Red Garter, though, stood out with its seductive neon call. The glowing sign, in the shape of a female leg clad in a black fishnet stocking held by a red garter, had a message printed below that suggested massages, though the leg suggested much more. The street was crowded, mostly with men, American and European men in the country on business. Some had a girl hanging onto an arm, a girl one would not take home to meet parents, a girl who suggested the same message as the neon sign.

Lyle stumbled out of the Red Garter Parlor into the heat and humidity of the night and headed across the street to a pub for more drink, something to take his mind off the dark-haired, caramel-skinned beauty he wanted to spend the entire night with rather than the few minutes allotted. Or was she a beauty beneath all that makeup—exaggerated eyelashes and bright red lipstick behind which flashed pearly white teeth? Did it make any difference to the men who visited her? Lyle had insisted, but she'd turned a cold shoulder. Her smile vanished, and she'd threatened to summon the bouncer if he didn't leave immediately.

As he bumbled his way out through the red-carpeted foyer lined with red and gold wallpaper, he heard her voice in the inner parts of the parlor beckoning the next man. "Hello, honey. Welcome to the Red Garter."

He crossed the dirty street, dodging around some unrecognizable blob, and staggered through the open front door of the pub, where he fell against the well-worn bar and ordered whiskey—not his first shot of the night. The bottle and a convenient woman; that's all he needed. Charts, compass, whiz wheels, and plotting courses guiding an aircrew across vast expanses of nothingness were far off in another world, a world only vaguely remembered through the haze of the evening.

He tossed the drink down his throat and turned to exit the pub, took a few faltering, stumbling steps, and bumped into another American, causing him to spill his drink.

"Pardon me," Lyle mumbled before taking another unsteady step toward the door.

"Hey, fella! You owe me a drink."

Lyle continued toward the door.

The red-haired man, about the same height and build as Lyle, wearing a white shirt with collar open, grabbed him by the shoulder and spun him around.

Lyle stumbled, his arms flinging like those of a rag doll.

"I said you owe me a drink!"

"I don't owe you nothin'."

"Wanna bet?"

"Yeah."

"This is your last chance. You gonna buy me another drink?"

Lyle started to turn away, but the man threw a punch that landed on his chin and sent him reeling backward, desperately grabbing for anything with which to steady himself. But his hands found nothing, and the crowd parted, clearing a path for the tumbling, backward-falling man, who crashed back first onto a round table.

The offended man approached Lyle where he lay sprawled on top of the table and declared, "Now, how 'bout that drink, you bum?"

Lyle struggled to his feet and took a swing at the

fellow—a wide, wild punch that missed its target. The man stepped forward to throw his own punch, but Lyle caught him with a swing from the other hand, the blow sending the fellow backward. The man then grabbed a chair and began swinging and jabbing it. Lyle dodged each move, then picked up a chair of his own, and the men went at each other like two drunken, chair-wielding lion tamers. Chair legs made contact, again and again, shattering and splintering from the blows. The pub patrons stood back along the walls, giving the men room and staying clear of stray punches and chairs. Both men dropped what remained of their weapons and began jabbing and punching and dancing around each other, like two clumsy boxers. More punches and jabs missed than connected. Their hair fell into their eyes and sweat soaked their clothes and dripped from their faces.

Four police officers burst through the open door, subdued the men, and handcuffed them before escorting them out into the night and to waiting cars, which whisked them away.

The patrons ebbed back toward the middle of the room. Talk and laughter gradually filled the air again, and the owner and barkeeper picked up pieces of broken chairs, while the evening went on as if nothing unusual had happened.

In the meantime, Ed Butz prowled the city on

his own mission—one distinctly different from Lyle's. He searched the corners, cubbyholes, and shadows, and pumped people for information, specifically information concerning the mysterious, shadowy man, officials, airplane parts, and other goods. Ed Butz worked his magic: conning, cajoling, and prying.

Ed returned late, about midnight, carrying a plain brown cardboard box tied shut with twine, a box obviously with weight to it. It contained cigars, pipe tobacco, a carburetor for the S-42 engines, and tropical shirts.

On hearing Ed unlocking his door, Captain Williams stepped into the hallway and asked, "Butz, whaddaya have there?"

"Cigars. And shirts. Tourists shirts."

"What are we gonna do with them?"

"Smoke them, what else?"

The captain shook his head. "No, the shirts."

"Oh, we could wear them."

"You're kidding, right?"

"It's up to you."

"They may be handy for trade, for bartering."

"They may. We end up in the bush somewhere, we could trade them for food or whatever. Oh yeah, I got a carburetor too. Fits the Hornet engine, same model as on the plane."

"How did you get that?"

Ed made no response to that question. Instead, he said, "I did get some information on Holtz. Verifies what the navy captain told us. He's a Nazi and has an accomplice, and they have an airplane hidden somewhere, probably at a remote strip in the jungle. It's a single-engine job. It's been seen flying in and out of the area the last few days. Gotta be the plane we've been seein', that Messerschmitt 108.

"His sidekick is a fella named Hans Frederick," Ed continued. "They split up after that trouble in Guatemala but joined up again a couple weeks ago in Colombia. Like Captain Spencer said, seems they really did kill a fellow who got in their way."

"Good work, Butz."

"Oh, and I did hear that Ellison got into some trouble. I'm not a stool pigeon, but he'll no doubt call you for help. He's in jail. Just wanted to give you a heads-up."

The captain's eyes widened. "Jail?"

"Yeah. A fight in a tavern."

"Great! I had hoped he'd work out, but I guess not. Seems he can't let go of old habits."

"We gonna leave him?"

"As far as I'm concerned, we are. He was warned."

"How about navigation?"

"We'll get along. Won't be the ideal situation, but

we can make do. Harold can work that direction-finding radio, and Jack is good with charts."

"I guess we can. Gonna call the police station tonight?"

"I suppose I better, so I'll have the details to relay to the old man in the morning."

"Oh, one more thing. He was seen coming out of a place called the Red Garter Parlor. You know what that had to be."

"Wonderful! One more of his vices to deal with."

~

Next morning, the captain visited Lyle at the police station. With both hands, Lyle hung on to the bars of the cell door as Captain Williams offered stern words. Two other men in the cell, one a European, the other a Recife native, disheveled and hung over from a night out, sat on the floor, backs against the stone wall, eyes closed. At the captain's words, their eyes opened slowly. "I warned you, Mister Ellison," he said.

"It wasn't my fault. The other fella started the fight."

"You were drunk as a skunk."

"That has nothing to do with it."

"That has everything to do with it. If you'd have stayed sober, you'd have had no trouble. And you were seen coming out of that red-light house. Fine example for Caribbean Air."

"That, my good man, was a massage parlor."

"Sure. We know the type of massages they give."

"Well, are you going to bail me out?"

"Not personally, but I called the office this morning, the main office in New York City, and talked to the old man. He's wiring the money to get you out and to pay for damages in the tavern. It's between you and him to work out a deal to pay him back.

"More news," the captain continued. "You're staying on. The old man said to give you one more chance. If it was up to me, I'd keep my word and leave you right here, but once more and even he won't help you. Got that?"

"Yeah, I got that."

Captain Williams waited until the money for the fine arrived, and then he accompanied Lyle in a cab back to the hotel. "If this was the military, I'd confine you to quarters," the captain said. "But since it's not, all I can do is suggest you stay close. And no drinking!"

"Yes sir!" Lyle mockingly stood at attention and saluted.

The captain just gritted his teeth and walked away.

The men spent the rest of the day going over

the airplane thoroughly, inspecting every fastener and connection from nose to tail. They examined control cables and attachment points closely, opened the engine cowls and inspected each engine for loose connections and oil and fuel leaks. Each seventy-four-gallon oil tank was filled to the correct level, and Ed supervised the plane's refueling, inspecting the fuel for water and other contaminants. The S-42 featured single-point refueling which allowed all eight tanks to be filled from one filling port in the center of the wing rather than filling each tank separately. When finished, the men had confidence that the plane was in top condition for its flight to Salvador and then on to Rio de Janeiro—a full day's flying.

Two navy guards were present the entire time to ensure no unauthorized person approached the plane.

After the evening meal, Captain Williams, Jack, and Harold ventured out into the city. They walked down the narrow stone streets, where pedestrians mixed with horse-drawn carts and automobiles and the Zeppelin trams rumbled back and forth. They partook of some street food called *bolo de rolo*—a dessert similar to a jelly roll cake, made from multiple rolled layers of guava cake and filled with guava jam. They listened to street musicians and watched people dance. The women twirled, their skirts swirling, with men in light-colored pants tand shirts, some wearing narrow ties, others with open collars. They remained in the good part of town, not venturing into the area of the Red Garter and other shady establishments. Even so, a familiar figure caught their attention as he moved, shadow-like, in and out of the crowd. The man wore a hat pulled down low, but in the glimpses they managed, they saw the horn-rimmed glasses and the telltale scar.

Harold pulled his pipe from his mouth. "It's him!"

"Try to keep him in our sights," the captain said.

"I'll cross to the other side of the street and run on ahead," Jack said, "then I'll double back on this side. Maybe we can trap him."

The men walked quickly, deliberately, moving in and out of groups of people and cutting around couples holding hands, searching as they went for the low-worn hat and the deep scar. Even faster, they walked, searching frantically, not wanting the man to escape. Jack, having run ahead, closed in, approaching the captain and Harold, the noose tightening on the shadowy man. Jack caught a glimpse of him and began to run. He cut between couples and dodged around groups, his shoes pounding on the pavement, then he ran through the middle of a group of dancers and stopped abruptly, face-to-face with the captain and Harold.

Jack looked around. "Where'd he go?"

"There!" Harold pointed to a man running toward an arm of the river that curved its way through the city.

All three took off in pursuit, but the man had too much of a head start, and before they could reach him, he jumped into a waiting boat and roared off into the night.

"Get a boat!" Harold yelled.

Jack looked up and down the river. "Where? There's no boats here. There's not even a dock."

"He's gone," the captain said. "The city's like Venice with all the waterways crisscrossing the place. He could be in another part of town already."

Harold relit his pipe. "He can't escape us forever."

~

Before dawn the next day, the men gathered in the restaurant for breakfast. While the others enjoyed eggs, bacon, and toast, Lyle had only coffee, and he spent a lot of the time holding his head, not from alcohol but from a migraine. After breakfast, they returned to their rooms, where a navy guard still stood in the hallway, packed their bags and flight gear, and headed out for the short walk to the harbor.

Captain Williams stopped at the desk. "We're leaving now. I'll sign whatever paperwork you have."

"No paperwork," the man replied.

"All right, thank you. I do want to say this is the finest accommodations we've had on our trip. It's a first-rate place."

"Thank you, sir. You men have a safe flight."

The mayor, his assistant, and Captain Spencer greeted the men at the dock. Captain Williams sent the crew on to begin preflight checks while he chatted with the officials. The mayor, a short, thin fellow, was an easy talking and relaxed kind of fella. He wore the usual light-colored suit, as well as a straw hat. His assistant, also thin and standing several inches taller than the mayor, wore a light-colored suit but remained bareheaded. He fidgeted and continually puffed on his cigarette.

"It's nice to meet you, mayor," the captain said. "The hospitality here has been wonderful. We haven't been treated better anywhere else."

"I'm very glad to hear that. It is our goal to accommodate you and your airline. We look forward to the service you will provide to Recife."

"Yes," said the assistant, "we look forward to you bringing in business. Yes, the airplane is the way of the future, and we want to be a part of it, the future."

After a round of shaking hands and well-wishing, Captain Williams turned to board the plane.

"Have a safe flight," Captain Spencer said. "Keep

your guard up for the men we talked about. If you have a problem, contact our ship by radio."

"As a matter of fact, we saw one of the men last night—Holtz. We tried to corner him, but he got away by boat into the city."

"We'll do a check of the city, but chances are he's miles away by now. A small plane was sighted last night flying away from the airstrip just outside town."

A crowd of people lined the waterfront, as usual, to watch the plane take off. After patiently waiting and watching, they weren't disappointed as the machine gracefully ascended into the sky, made a wide turn to the north and then back south toward the harbor. Jack flew, right hand easily yet firmly on the control wheel, his left hand on the overhead throttles. Below, the strip of white, sandy beach glistened in the early morning sun, and the waterways that laced the city sparkled. The Zeppelin trams were running, shuffling people about the city, and cars and horse-drawn carts filled the streets as the busy day began.

After the flyover of the harbor, Jack turned the plane on course for Salvador, taking a path that followed the coast for the two-and-a-half-hour flight. From there it would be on to Rio de Janeiro for the night.

Once established in cruise flight, the men began to chat.

"Butz," said Jack, "you get out last night?"

"Yeah."

"Get anything good?"

"Cigars. Chocolate. Information."

"What information?"

"That load of coffee we're to pick up in Belém on the return flight. We need to check it close, cut open a few bags."

"Why?"

"Contraband hidden in it."

"Such as?"

"Probably drugs."

Jack's eyebrows rose. "Drugs?"

"Yeah. There's an underground market for certain drugs in the United States. It may be hidden from most of us, but it's there. And that's one area I steer well clear of."

"Yes," Lyle said through the intercom. "Like Butz says, it's underground. But there's a certain amount of people who partake. Guess it's spreading through the middle-class. I encountered drugs in Morocco and Algeria. I stay away from that stuff—it's only alcohol for me. And women."

"Also, there may be money hidden in the coffee," Ed continued. "I can't verify any of this, but we need to be alert for it and check it. We get caught with contraband onboard, that may well be the end of

Caribbean Airways."

"That may be the whole idea," Harold said. "The Nazis want to get us out of the way, so they can take over the routes, and that may be a good way to do it."

Jack turned to Captain Williams and without using the intercom, privately asked, "Think there's any truth to all that?"

"I don't know. But for our own protection, we better assume there is."

The relatively short flight to Salvador went smoothly. The vast green expanse of the land below glided by beneath the wings, the ocean off to the left, the morning air smooth, and the sky cloudless, a perfect day for flight.

Under Harold's tutoring, Lyle incorporated the direction-finding radio. He turned knobs to home in on the Adcock station in Salvador, while double-checking the invisible waves with his trusted means of navigation. He plotted and calculated and drew lines on the chart spread out on his table, then checked against the radio. The headings were the same. Still, he didn't fully trust the black box of wires and tubes.

The facilities in Salvador were in place just as Captain Spencer had indicated, and the men were treated to a good meal in addition to the usual meeting and greeting by city officials. The plane took on more fuel, and by early afternoon, was off to Rio de Janeiro, a flight where, once again, the men would generally follow the coastline. The afternoon cumulus was building up, and the subsequent vertical air currents made for a bouncy flight—all part of flying in the tropics. The men, used to the air currents, remained relaxed. Harold, who was gaining more confidence in flying, only grabbed the edge of his table during the more severe bumps.

About an hour into the flight, Ed said through the intercom, "Look, a ship at ten o'clock."

"What are you doing looking out the window?" Jack asked. "You're supposed to be facing the other way."

"Hey, staring at these gauges makes my eyes go crazy after a while. I need to look at something else now and then."

Jack leaned over to look out the portside window. "A cargo ship?"

"Looks like it might be," Lyle said from his station in the cabin. "Giving it a look through the glasses right now."

Harold got up from his seat and knelt behind the pilots to get a good look at the vessel. "Don't mean to get in your way," he said before putting the pipe back into his mouth and giving it a puff.

"You've got a better view here," Jack said. "You're not in our way."

"A military ship?" Harold asked.

"It may be a navy vessel," Lyle said over the intercom. "I can't quite make out details."

"Shall we divert course to get closer?" asked Jack. "Might be Captain Spencer's ship."

The captain nodded. "Sure, we've got plenty of fuel. Harold, get back to the radio, see if you can raise anyone on the boat."

"Yes sir, I'll see what I can do."

The ship proved to be farther away than it appeared. The men flew on, only slowly covering the expanse of water between them and the mystery vessel. Harold tried all the marine frequencies and could raise no one.

Finally Lyle said, "I think I can make out what the boat is. It's military, all right. And it's German."

"German!" Harold exclaimed.

"Yes. I see the German flag, that swastika flag."

"No wonder I can't raise them on the radio," Harold said. "Either they don't understand me or they don't want to respond."

"They don't want to respond," the captain said. "At least some crew on any ship knows a little bit of English. Jack, go ahead and give them a buzz job."

"Yes sir!"

Jack altered course even more toward the east in order to intercept the ship and at the same time began a gradual descent. The men were going to leave the

Germans no doubt that they'd been seen. Slowly the gap closed, the ship became larger and details clearer. The long ship, a cruiser of the Reichsmarine, sat low in the water. A single smokestack jutted skyward near the middle of the ship, providing escape for the diesel-engine exhaust. Three large guns were mounted in a turret near the bow with the same arrangement near the stern. A Nazi flag flew from the tall mast midship that thrust up from a spiderweb of rigging. A biplane on floats rested atop a platform aft of the smokestack, along with a hoist to lower and retrieve it from the water.

Then they were close enough to see men on the deck.

"Take it on down," the captain said. "And fly right over the top of them."

Jack had a big grin on his face as he lowered the nose of the plane and aimed right for the ship. It now loomed large in the windscreen, the Nazi flags seen plainly, flying from the bow, stern, and mast.

Jack leveled off just above the height of the ship and called to Ed for full rich mixture, then he reached up to the overhead control console and pushed the throttles and propellers full forward. The ship flashed beneath the wings in a gray blur. Jack then pulled up into a left-hand steep-bank turn to come around again, easing back the throttles to go slower, so the crew could get a good look at the ship. After crossing abeam the bow, Jack continued the turn, then leveled and flew parallel to the ship. The men scurrying around on the deck were easily visible.

Suddenly, Captain Williams shouted, "They're shooting! Go! Get away!"

Jack pushed the throttle and propeller levers full forward again and, using what altitude they had, went into a shallow dive to build speed as machine gun bullets filled the air and the antiaircraft guns turned to track the fleeing plane. They flew quickly out of range of the machine guns and were too low for antiaircraft fire.

Ed chuckled. "Guess we riled them up a bit."

Jack grinned. "I guess so. There's no doubt in their minds we know where they are. Lyle, get us back on course."

"Will do."

"Ed, check for any damage," Captain Williams said.

"Yes sir, Captain."

"Radio, contact the navy vessel that's near Recife. We need to relay the position of the German boat. When you make contact, connect me."

"Roger. Will do."

Jack chuckled. "All those years in the military, this is the first time I've been shot at."

The captain nodded. "Me too."

"Captain," Harold called. "I have Captain

Spencer on the radio. You're connected."

"Captain Spencer, Max Williams with Caribbean Airways survey flight."

"Go ahead, Williams."

"We just encountered a German naval vessel. We went down low for a look and received gunfire from them."

"Are you damaged?"

"I don't believe so. A crewman is making an inspection now."

"We'd received word a German ship was prowling the region, but it wasn't confirmed until now. Thanks for passing along the information. Can you give an exact position?"

"Navigator, give Captain Spencer the location of the German boat."

After Lyle was done conferring with Captain Spencer, the captain said, "Captain Williams, you and your men stay alert. And I trust you're flying away from that boat now."

"Yes sir. He's already several miles behind us."

"Good. Keep it that way."

"Yes sir."

Ed returned to the flight deck and reported he had found no damage. Captain Williams, who relieved Jack of flying duties so he could have a break, guided the plane back on its course for Rio where they would soon follow the coast southward again. The land to starboard guided them; the water to port offered a place to land if needed. The men took turns going back to the cabin to stretch out, relax, and walk back and forth to refresh before returning to their respective crew stations for more hours of monitoring gauges, working flight controls, and tuning and turning knobs.

Jack was flying when Rio de Janeiro came into sight in the late afternoon. The city spread out over the hilly coast, the green hills peeking through fleeting white clouds.

"Wow!" Jack, who despite the captain's ban on idle talk at low altitude, could not restrain himself. "That's some city. It goes on and on."

"At least a million people," the captain said.

"I don't think we better do a flyover," Jack said. "There's a lot of hills, and the clouds are hiding some of them."

The clouds scooted by, some wispy, some solid, and the green hills, sparkling water, and the rows and rows of building-lined streets came in and out of view. Rio de Janeiro sent out an alluring call, a seductive invitation to the men to come down and stay a while.

"Lost the Adcock," Lyle called.

Harold tuned his own navigation radio and

listened. "Yeah, no signal. We had it earlier; it was working fine. The hills! That must be it! The hills are blocking the signal."

"That magic box is no good now," Lyle declared. "But that's all right; I'll get us right to the harbor." Lyle gave a compass heading for the pilots and divided his attention between his chart and the outside view as he searched for landmarks.

Jack reduced engine power and adjusted the propellers. "Prepare for prelanding checks. Navigator, help us identify the correct harbor for landing."

"Yes sir. Continue on your present heading and maintain at least three thousand feet to clear the terrain."

"How much room will that give?"

"At least six hundred feet."

"Looking for a big hill, are we?" Jack asked Lyle.

"Affirmative. Sugarloaf. It'll be easy to identify. It'll be on the south side of the harbor entrance."

Jack nodded. "Captain, help me look for the correct harbor."

Jack continued on course, all eyes on board looking for the big, wide harbor with the 2,330-foot-tall mountain called Sugarloaf as the prominent landmark. Jack split his time looking outside and scanning the gauges inside, eyes in constant motion, his hands and feet on the controls, making small, smooth corrections to keep the plane on course.

"Sugarloaf will be dead ahead," Lyle said.

"Roger," Jack said.

"There it is." The captain pointed as a cloud cleared away, revealing the mountain.

"We'll fly past it, and then circle out over the ocean and land toward the harbor," Jack said.

Captain Williams agreed. "Good plan."

Lyle said, "We've got a crowd here. I can see them lining the harbor. They're waving at us."

Jack flew on until the famous mountain slid by off the port wing, then he made a sweeping turn out over the ocean, flew about five miles out, then turned inbound for final approach toward the harbor.

After the 180-degree turn, Jack descended, flaps lowered to slow the plane for landing. Last-minute checks were made. The plane continued to descend down a gradual path toward the water while the men scanned the area for boats and any obstructions that would interfere with landing. Jack worked the controls and kept his left hand on the overhead throttles ready to make adjustments to engine power. The brisk wind whipped and swirled around the hills, creating turbulence that extended out into the harbor and bounced the plane ever harder the lower it flew. A sudden strong gust lifted the port wing and tried to throw the plane off course, but Jack, now working the controls fore and aft and left and right in large movements, kept the plane level and the nose pointed in the right direction. The water came closer and closer, and Jack leveled off just above the waves. He worked hard to guide the machine, making near full deflection of the controls to counter the gusty wind, but he held it off and let the plane slow even more. It settled onto the water with a thud, and they were no longer flying.

Jack guided the plane slowly further into the harbor, where a dock and ground crew, ready to secure the plane with ropes, awaited them. He carefully maneuvered to stay clear of the rowboats and sailing boats that filled the harbor. After they passed, the boats then trailed behind the plane, the procession resembling a mother duck followed by her ducklings.

After the postlanding checks had been made, the five crewmen, upon reminder by Captain Williams, tidied their uniforms and then exited the aircraft.

A small delegation of local officials met them.

"Welcome to Rio de Janeiro!" exclaimed a slightly heavy man dressed in a white suit and hat.

Captain Williams smiled. "Thank you. And Caribbean Airways thanks you for your cooperation. The facilities here look to be first-rate."

"Thank you. We wish to work with the airline as closely as we can. It should provide a valuable service to the region." The man then introduced the rest of the delegation and indicated the Caribbean Air crew would be taken by car to a hotel provided by the city. A car and driver would be available anytime they needed it and could be summoned by telephone. The man then indicated two armed police officers. "There will be a guard posted around the clock to protect your airplane," the man said. "Captain Spencer of the U. S. Navy did tell you about the guard, did he not?"

"He did," said Captain Williams. "He indicated your police force was trustworthy."

"Good. Now let's get you men to the hotel."

Air Racing

Those who could afford it paid fifty cents to enter the airport grounds. For special treatment, refreshments, and premium seating, the affluent paid two dollars fifty. Thousands of people paid the price and milled about the grounds, taking in sights and sounds. Those without the money stood outside the airport wherever they could find a spot—along the road, side streets, fields—in order to catch a glimpse of the brightly colored, powerful racing planes as they roared through the air.

Mechanics clamored over the planes, tuning the powerful engines, checking and tightening linkages, cables, nuts, and bolts, preparing the machines for competition. Exhibitors and food vendors hawked their wares, the whole affair taking on a carnival atmosphere. A dangerous carnival. The racing planes, huge, powerful engines stuffed into tiny airframes, roared full throttle fifty feet above the ground around pylons marking the course. People looked upward, shading their eyes with their hands as the planes zoomed past and into the pylon turns. Wingtip to wingtip they flew, skimming the earth, dicing for position. Oil flowed from an ailing engine, covering the plane with the black liquid as it pulled out of the race and quickly landed. Flames shot from an engine as it exploded from overstress. The pilot put the plane down in a cloud of dust and flying grass and dirt. He threw open the canopy and ran from the inferno. The remaining planes pushed their limits, straining to cross the finish line first.

Aviation was still new, thrilling, and thousands wanted to participate, even as spectators.

Chapter Seven

The next morning on the way to breakfast, Ed pulled Captain Williams aside and said, "I got out for a bit last night and got the information you wanted. The police officers guarding the plane are on the up-and-up. Four officers, two shifts, all four good men that can be trusted."

The captain nodded. "After you left last night, I got on the horn to the man Captain Spencer told me about. He also assured me we're in good hands."

At breakfast, all five men agreed to use the car and driver, see the sights, and take a day to relax from the long hours of flying. Dressed in civilian clothes, the men counted among the tourists, probing the sights and sounds, as well as the smells from the cafés and markets, much of it unfamiliar, strange, and exotic.

They mingled with the people—natives, tourists, and businesspeople—as they moved in and out of shops, buildings, and cafés. As in the other cities, hand-drawn carts, horse-drawn carts, and cars shared the narrow pavements, the traditional past meeting the progressive present. The meeting was not always amicable. Horns honked at the carts, urging them to clear the way for the faster automobiles, the present sweeping away the past as it forged ahead.

In addition to wheeled transportation, pedestrians crowded the sidewalks—dark-skinned Brazilian natives and pale-skinned Americans and Europeans. Some of the natives carried loads on their shoulders, carrying wares to the open markets and traded wares coming home. Light-colored shirts and pants were common, as well as wide-brimmed hats, all to protect from the blazing sun. The Americans and Europeans, the tourists, dressed in finery. Men in suits and women in dresses with necklaces, bracelets, and makeup, gawked in curiosity at the native life as it struggled to make a daily living. Those struggling were oblivious to international events and progress, including airplanes, and they ignored the curious looks of the intruders, intent on their daily struggle to survive.

The men wandered slowly through the narrow cobblestone side streets where open-air markets were set up in relative safety from the heavy traffic of the main thoroughfares. Goods to attract tourists as well as locals covered tables under white canvas awnings. Featured were dry-cured cigars—smaller and cheaper than conventional cigars and with a spicy taste. The gemstones in jewelry and decorative objects glistened in the light, and ceramic figurines of mythological Brazilian characters stood silently in rows. Woven straw baskets were common and hung from the poles supporting the awnings. The baskets came in all sizes, from not much bigger than a man's hand to those that could carry a day's supply of groceries. Then there were treats: *Goiabada*, or guava paste, that came in tins; *Castanha do Para*, or Brazil nuts, displayed in bulk in weather-worn wooden crates; and good Brazilian coffee.

In this narrow street, the wealthy white travelers who'd discovered this area off the beaten path meandered through the markets. The women, with their slouch hats defending them from the sun, and the men, in their suits, ties, and fedoras, looked upon the scene with both intrigue and condescension, as if they were watching primates in a zoo. Still, they snatched up the trinkets and crafts. The native Brazilians knew the visitors were suckers, not as smart as their smugness suggested.

Christ the Redeemer, a ninety-eight-foot tall

statue of Jesus with arms outstretched, overlooked the city from atop the twenty-three hundred-foot Corcovado Mountain. The statue, even more prominent than Sugarloaf, was lit at night, always all-seeing and all-knowing, guarding the people in the city below.

Further down the street, the men came to the food vendors grilling exotic dishes on portable grills. The smells drifted through the area, spices and cooking meat calling to the palate.

"Hey, what's that?" Jack pointed to some unrecognizable food a street vendor was turning over on his grill. "Smells pretty good, kind of like grilled steak."

"You don't know?" Ed asked.

"If I did, would I be asking?"

"It's capybara."

"What's that?"

"A type of rat."

Jack grimaced. "Disgusting!"

Ed grinned. "I'm sure it's an acquired taste."

"I have no interest in acquiring it."

"Maybe you'd like some *buchada*."

"And what's that?"

"Goat stomach stuffed with kidneys, liver, and whatever other kind of innards are handy."

Jack screwed up his face in disgust. "I'm gonna

get sick."

Ed laughed. Harold turned a little green.

Jack posed the perfect question. "So you've tried this stuff, Butz?"

"Oh, hell no! You think I'm crazy?"

After wandering through the downtown markets, the men had the driver take them to a beach. They rode in comfort in the Checker Cab down tree-lined streets where they shared the road with the usual array of automobiles and street cars, as well as buses. The buses, often traveling in pairs, were full of the tourists being shuttled to the next part of town to see the sights, buy souvenirs, and gawk at the Brazilian people. They passed stately stone buildings that sported domes, turrets, and columns. In the numerous small parks and along the roadside were topiaries trimmed in the shapes of animals and geometric designs. One vast long hedge along the road was trimmed to look like a stone wall. The spires of Catholic churches dotted the skyline, some with a single steeple, some with twin spires reaching skyward, beseeching the heavens. In the middle of a roundabout stood another statue of Jesus, arms outstretched, brilliant in the bright sunshine. In the distance, Sugarloaf stood majestically over it all.

The men stopped at Copacabana Beach, a wide, expansive crescent of soft sand warmed by the blazing sun. Being a weekday, the beach wasn't crowded, just a handful of people here and there: some walked together in couples or groups; some strolled alone, seemingly deep in thought; some lay on towels on the sand, and some swam in the warm tropical water, wearing the latest in swimwear. Men wore one-piece bathing suits, the legs mid-thigh-length, and the new women's suits mimicked the men's, made of stretch material with legs slightly shorter than those of the men's suits. People of all shapes, sizes, and ages were enjoying a day in paradise. The green hills that surrounded the area, playing hide-and-seek with the clouds, provided stark contrast to the barren sand.

The driver waited as the men piled out of the car and strolled onto the sand. Jack removed his shoes and socks, rolled up his pants legs and, feeling the softness and warmth, exclaimed, "Wow! This feels great! I think I could spend all day here."

"Me too!" Lyle's gaze followed a pair of dark-skinned women walking out toward the water. "I don't think I'm ever gonna leave."

Harold chuckled. "Not the sand that's got your eye, is it?"

"Hell, no."

"Be careful of the women you meet," the captain said. "And the places you meet them."

"We're only gonna be here a couple of days," Lyle

pointed out. "I ain't gonna get attached."

"That's what I'm concerned about."

"Aw, don't get excited. I won't cause you and your morals any more trouble."

"I trust that you won't."

At that moment, Nassau seemed a million miles distant. They still had to fly to Buenos Aires, and from there, even with the fast plane they were flying, it would still take five days to make the return trip. Five days if all went smoothly. They had to stop for cargo in Belém—for the coffee that would eventually go to Miami. It would take time to load it, and, due to the information Ed Butz had gathered, the men would need to spend time inspecting it closely. The trip could easily turn into a week. But now all was forgotten as the men strolled the beach. The sounds of the waves created a serene rhythm as they rolled in and out, slapping and lapping at the sand, in and out, back and forth.

~

Since the men planned to remain another night, Ed and Lyle both took advantage and ventured out into the fading evening light. The heat and humidity were still oppressive even though the sun had set. The street life was just getting started. Musicians tuned instruments, and people began to fill the sidewalks. Families with children, groups of men and women, single people, and couples hand-in-hand, strolled slowly along, all looking for relief and entertainment in the coming darkness.

Despite the stern warning from Captain Williams, as well as Lyle's own vow to cause no trouble, he found himself wandering around the Lapa neighborhood, that region downtown near the aqueduct, the red-light district that beckoned with vices such as gambling, drugs, and women. Tipsy from an excess of alcohol, in which he'd indulged at a local establishment, he now ambled down the street where women strolled alone, leaned against walls, and hung out of second-floor windows. The women, dark-haired and exotic, stirred his imagination. He spoke with one of them, talking low, close in, with hushed voice, and then followed her into a dingy building, its dim hallway littered with trash. Other women walked in and out, some with a man, some alone. The voices of a man and woman arguing came from behind a closed door at the far end of the hallway.

Ed also prowled the night, but he ignored the women. He had more pressing things for which to search: cigars, engine parts, information, all more important than the women who strolled the streets looking for men desperate enough to part with their money. Ed had deals to make.

Jack was still awake when Ed returned to the hotel and on hearing his door open, he opened his own door and caught Ed's attention.

"Well, Butz, how was your night out?"

"Productive. Got some good cigars. I checked them out this time; wasn't gonna get taken like that last time. Got some hooch, too. It may be handy for bartering. And some chocolate; it may be a handy barter item too. Also another carburetor that fits the Hornet engine and some parts. And some more information."

"What kind of information?"

"Reaffirms what I learned last night. What Captain Spencer said is true. The government and the police are on the up-and-up, and we can trust them. They've done what they can to discourage the Nazis. But it's a big city with over a million people, so they can blend in."

"What about the fella I overheard Captain Spencer talking about?"

"He's legit. He's actually a navy officer of Latin descent, so he blends in and always wears civilian clothes. He's found no problems yet with the local government or the police."

"Think there's any need to post one of our own men with the plane?"

"In my opinion, I don't think so. Of course, it can't hurt. Maybe tomorrow night one of us should stay with the plane. Just for insurance."

"I've been wondering about Japanese activity. Do they have a presence in the area?"

"Yes. Here and in Panama. Our military, as well as the local authorities, are keeping tabs on them."

"Are they working together? The Nazi Germans and the Japanese?"

"Not sure. They do have a common goal to take over the Western Hemisphere, so I'm sure they cooperate, at least to a degree."

Jack sighed. "The world situation is even worse than I realized. I may get called back to the military. I just don't know what's going to happen, but it can't be good."

Japan had taken over Manchuria, renaming it Manchukuo, and were heading south and had breached parts of the Great Wall. Japan officially declared that it had special responsibilities in East Asia and it opposed China receiving aid from Western countries. Japan felt that it was its duty to see order restored in China, a country which had been composed of various factions led by warlords, as well as the Communists who were opposing the Nationalists led by Chiang Kai-Shek. In the meantime in Japan, the leaders were mentally preparing the population for a war with the United States.

The next morning, all the men met for breakfast except Lyle, who remained in bed in sleep so deep he was miles away from the memories of the night before and the accompanying pain in his head. All that bliss came to an abrupt end with a pounding on the door. Holding his head, he stumbled out of bed, fumbled his way to the door, and opened it a crack.

"Morning, sunshine!" Ed exclaimed.

"Butz, you no good son-of-a-bitch," Lyle managed to get out from between his parched lips.

"Ellison, I know what happened last night. I'm not a stool pigeon, but if you get in trouble and the captain presses me, I'll have to tell him."

"What are you talking about, Butz?"

"The hooker. And the excess booze."

"Yeah, well, what about them?"

"If I know about it, then others know, too. If word gets back to Williams, you're in big trouble; you know that."

"So what do you want, Butz? Money?"

"I don't want anything. I'm just giving you a heads-up."

"Well now, ain't that generous."

"I recommend you clean up and shape up real quick or the captain will come down on you."

"I will. Just leave me alone."

~

The men spent the day inspecting the plane under Ed's direction. His coveralls became soaked with sweat, and sweat ran down his forehead into his eyes. He constantly wiped it away, creating smudges from his grime-covered hands. But he was in his element, doing what he enjoyed, hands deep in mechanical parts, working his magic, massaging, manipulating, and adjusting machinery, coaxing it to perform flawlessly.

After the day of sweating and laboring on the plane, the men returned to the hotel where they cleaned up, and then had dinner together in the restaurant around the corner. The small establishment was cozy, homey, with a counter of worn dark wood and red leather-topped stools, round, mounted on shiny silver posts and able to rotate 360 degrees. The men sat at the counter, ate sandwiches and drank coffee and chatted about the sights they'd seen, as well as what they planned to do when they got back home. Home was days away, yet the men's minds were beginning to bend in that direction. Thoughts of familiar surroundings and feelings of nervous anticipation and longing began to take root. Such thoughts and feelings would grow larger as the men drew closer to Nassau.

"What are you fellas going to do first when we get to Nassau?" asked Harold.

"I'm going to see my woman," said Captain Williams. "During the time I've been gone, she's moved to Nassau for a teaching job. Didn't even get to help her move in. That was disappointing."

"She flew on Caribbean Air, didn't she?" Jack asked.

"Her first commercial flight, yeah, and I wasn't there for that either. But it'll be good to see her again."

"I hear you and Gail are going out," Ed said to Jack.

"Well, not yet, but we plan to. I promised I'd see her and we'd go somewhere, do something, and I'd take her for a ride on that motorcycle I bought from you."

"You got a good machine there," Ed said. "I gave you a great deal, you know."

Jack smiled. "Time will tell, Butz. I haven't ridden it enough to get it fully checked out."

"Hey, it won't give you no trouble."

"Well, if it does, I know where to take it for a refund."

"Jack, how about that Chinese girl?" Lyle asked. "You never did tell me if you were seeing her."

"I told you, Max and I see her at the restaurant. That's all there is to it. And she's Chinese American."

"Well, sorry I didn't use the correct terminology,"

Lyle said sarcastically. "But I hear you and her have spent some time together."

"Nothing more than conversation at the restaurant. I don't know where you got your information, but there's nothing to it." Jack, who was normally easygoing, began to get an edge to his voice.

"No need to get defensive unless you're trying to hide something. Captain, is Jack covering up details he doesn't want to share?"

"No, he's on the level. We usually get lunch at her folks' restaurant before the leg back to Nassau. Got great food there, and the owner is a wonderful fella."

"So you're saying Jack doesn't get anything there but a meal?"

"That's what I'm saying."

"Well, unless you two are hiding something, I've got my information wrong."

After a few moments of uneasy silence, Harold asked, "Ed, do you have a woman?"

"Naw, not really; I'm too busy for that."

"What about the girl in Miami?" asked Lyle.

"I don't have no regular girl."

"That's a good practice," Lyle said. "Regular girls tie a fella down."

"Well now, if I am seeing someone, she's more regular than the girls you visit. We're more friends than anything."

"So you're admitting you do see someone," Harold said.

"Take it however you want to. Yeah, I might take a notion to visit Miami sometime after we get back. And what about you, Harold? Seein' anyone?"

Harold looked down, hesitated, then said, "No, not anymore."

Harold had a steady woman until she broke things off. Due to his work, she claimed. All he could think about and talk about were radios and those invisible radio waves. He constantly spoke of frequencies and wavelengths and coils and tubes, all subjects foreign to her, though she asked him to explain. He tried. He explained, drew diagrams, tried to get the information in his head out to her, and the more he talked, the more excited he got about the subject. She decided he liked radios more than her. After the breakup, he left RCA for the job at Caribbean Airways. He needed a change, not just in jobs, but in surroundings, so a move from New York City to the Bahamas would provide just what he needed. John Trapp was delighted to hire Harold, who he considered a radio genius, and Harold welcomed the opportunity.

"Might be better off," Ed said. "I've not met one yet who I'd want to settle down with. Course, if the right one comes along, I suppose I'd get married."

Harold nodded. "Yeah, the right one. They're few and far between. If you find her, do her right. Don't let her go."

"Sounds like speaking from experience," Ed said.

Harold made no reply.

After the meal, Jack wandered off by himself to think. In addition to the discussion at mealtime, the Chinese couple he'd seen earlier in the lobby stirred up thoughts, and he wanted to be alone. He'd been successful at putting Sally out of his immediate thoughts, but she lingered in the far reaches, the image of her the last time he saw her in the dark behind the restaurant.

Her folks expected her to marry the Chinese American fellow she'd been seeing, and Jack knew, too, down deep, that his folks back home in Missouri would have a bit of hesitancy about her, a woman from a different culture, a different race. He knew they'd be polite; they'd treat her well, but when they had him aside, they'd question why he couldn't find a girl more like the girls on the neighboring farms. But he had no intention of moving back to Missouri, at least not back to the rural area, because aviation centered around the larger areas, cities like Kansas City, St. Louis, Chicago, and Atlanta. And the thought of midwestern winters was enough to keep him in the Caribbean region. Other than visits, he had no intention of returning to the hills.

He ran into Captain Williams on his way back to the hotel, and the men stopped to chat. "Getting some fresh air, Jack?"

"Yeah. And thinking some things over. You doing the same?"

"I guess I am. Been thinking about Jennifer and seeing her soon. You know it's time for her and I to settle down, and I'm ready. A little house, a woman to come home to, kids; it all sounds good to me. Never thought I'd feel that way, but I do. It's going to be so nice to travel a few minutes to see her instead of having to go to Miami. I'm looking forward to it. So are you thinking about Sally?"

"How'd you guess?"

"I know how much you like her. It shows."

"Yeah, well, I've been trying to forget about her."

"Maybe you shouldn't."

"Why? It won't work out for us, and she's got her mind made up."

"I wouldn't be too sure that she does."

"Why?"

"I've seen the way she looks at you, that's why."

"Really?"

"Yes, I've seen it, seen her looking at you with that look of admiration or respect when a woman likes a fella. Think about it, Jack."

The captain and Jack wandered back to the hotel and sat in the lobby, watching the people rather than sit in their rooms. Ed sauntered in and joined them, and they sat and watched the parade of people go back and forth—men, women, and families with children ranging from toddlers to teenagers.

Soon a familiar face appeared, trailing a cloud of pipe smoke.

"Hey, Harold!" Ed called.

Harold turned, slightly startled. "Oh, hey fellas." He paused.

"Where you headed?" Ed asked.

"Just out for a walk. Tired of sitting in the room."

"Well, be careful out there."

Harold just grinned from one corner of his mouth; the other corner clamped tight around his pipe.

"He's working out all right," Ed said. "Still a bit of a nervous fella, but he knows his radios. Actually, I don't think he's a bad navigator, either. Been picking it up from Lyle. Bet he and that radio could take over if he had to."

Jack agreed. "Yeah, he's worked out. Not quite as aloof as he was at first."

"I think he felt out of place," the captain said. "He's starting to get more comfortable. I have full confidence in him."

"One thing I haven't figured out," Ed said. "That little brown paper bag, the one he puts at his station on every flight. Never see him carry it off at the end of the flight. Wonder what's in it."

Jack grinned. "You don't know? Butz, I though you knew everything."

Ed chuckled. "That's just a rumor."

"That little brown paper bag always contains a peanut butter sandwich."

"What! A sandwich! I never see him eat it."

"He has his back to you."

"Yeah, but still …"

"I've seen him have that sandwich and a cup of coffee about ten o'clock every morning. Says he gets lightheaded if he doesn't eat something about that time."

"Where's he get it? The sandwich; how's he get one every day?"

"Says he stops at the nearest café and has one made."

Ed chuckled. "I'll be. Missed something right in front of me."

⁓

The men were a couple of hours into the eight-hour flight to Buenos Aires, Argentina, their southernmost point before they'd turn back toward home. Though the day had dawned clear, the air was turbulent, and cumulus clouds had already begun to build, unusual for so early in the day. The constant bouncing and jostling became more severe and threw the men against their safety belts. The bouncing wasn't steady or rhythmic, but erratic with occasional sudden, violent jolts thrown into the already uncomfortable ride. Though not fun, it was something the men had experienced before, so it caused no real alarm.

Harold, despite his gained flying confidence, grabbed the edge of his table at each jostle. Between the violent events, though, he rode the turbulence out like a pro.

The turbulence followed them the entire flight, beating them continuously, wearing on both the body and the mind. By the time the men landed in Buenos Aires, they were exhausted and in no mood for what lay ahead.

They flew just off the coast and past the harbor where docks reached out into the mouth of the Rio de la Plata. Oceangoing ships pulled away, headed for far-off locations, and ships entered the harbor, but the men couldn't find a dock for them, nor a marked landing lane. In addition to the large ships, some hauling cargo, others loaded with passengers, smaller boats, many of them steam-powered, chugged about, trailing long plumes of smoke that billowed out of their smokestacks. The waterfront was a maze of organized chaos as trucks and horse-drawn wagons crisscrossed paths, and people on foot and on bicycles navigated through the clutter and clamor. Warehouses lined the seafront, many of them with huge, refrigerated rooms storing meat ready for export that would make its way to the ships and then on to Europe. In addition to the meat, trucks and wagons loaded with sugar cane and wool made their way to the warehouses, where they'd be held until ready for shipment. Despite the approaching dusk, activity didn't slow.

Harold hadn't been able to tune in the Adcock radio, but as Buenos Aires got closer, he managed to raise someone on the maritime radio. All he could get from the fellow on the other end were vague, discombobulated instructions that were no help at all, leaving the men to their own devices for landing. Jack set the plane down well clear of the dock activity, then taxied in, maneuvering slowly around ships and small boats. Since he didn't know the depth of the water or if there were any submerged obstructions, he didn't dare go too far into the harbor. When he found a suitable spot, Ed deployed the anchor to hold the plane in place, and Harold called for a boat. The men waited. Harold called again. The sun was about to touch the western horizon. They'd have to spend the night in the plane if something didn't happen quickly.

Finally a small boat chugged out of the encroaching darkness toward them.

"Captain, think it's safe to leave the plane out here unattended?" Harold asked.

"No, I don't."

"I'll stay with it."

"No, Harold, it's my responsibility. I'll stay."

"But captain, you have things to do, like contact New York and Nassau and plan for our trip home. No, I'll stay."

"You sure?"

"Yes. Just get me some food and lots of water. I'm really thirsty."

Four of the crew climbed into the boat and made their way slowly to shore, then they followed the directions given by the boater to get to the nearby taxi stand. They weaved their way through the busy dockyard, dodging trucks and carts that darted about in a chaotic, random order. If there were any direction protocols, they weren't visible to the untrained eyes of the inexperienced.

Once safely clear of the docks, the men stood at the edge of a busy street filled with cars, the usual Model T and Model A Fords, as well as the Cadillacs and the Cords. The cars swerved around the two-wheeled horse-drawn carts, some with overly tall, spoked wheels. The trees lining the street swayed easily in the evening breeze. The men, overnight bags in hand, piled into a cab they hailed for the ride to the hotel. Though only a few blocks, it was too far to carry overnight bags. The cab turned onto another street, a boulevard with trees down the middle, and continued on to a roundabout with a statue of some local historic figure in the middle. The city was full of statues and fountains, statues of mythical characters as well as national heroes, all carved in white stone.

The open-air markets that lined the narrow side streets were closing for the day. The vendors tucked away goods they'd bring out in the light of the following day when people would haggle for the best prices, all beneath the canvas canopies. People lingered on street corners while others relished meals in the sidewalk cafés. The men wore coats despite the unseasonable heat, as it was illegal for them to be in public without one. Rather than suit coats, some men wore lightweight pajama jackets to remain comfortable.

The cab stopped in front of a battered building with a torn canvas canopy over the front entrance.

Jack frowned. "Is this the hotel?"

"Yes, this is it," replied the cabbie, a tall, skinny fellow with the sleeves of his white shirt rolled up in defiance of the coat order.

The four men exited the cab and stood looking at the building.

"What kind of a dump is this?" Lyle asked. "I've seen some pretty Spartan accommodations around the world, but this looks like it could be the worst."

The men stared at the three-story building. It had great areas of worn and faded stucco falling off it, and sagging, paint-chipped shutters framed dingy windows, one of which was broken.

"Reckon it's safe?" Jack asked. "Makes the hotel back in Belém look first-class."

"Doesn't look like it," Ed said. "Hell, even I'm afraid of what we might find inside."

The men entered through the scuffed and worn wooden door into the dim lobby. The desk clerk, a short, thin man with a thin mustache and thin lips, greeted them. Though he was unaware that the men from Caribbean Airways were coming, he was amiable, smiled a lot, and treated the men with gratitude. At least the hotel had that going for it. He pointed the men to the wooden stairway up to the second floor, and as they made their way up, each step creaked beneath their feet. The worn, sloping flooring of the hallway also creaked as they walked down it.

"At least no one can sneak up on us," Jack noted.

Lyle snorted. "About the only good thing about

this place."

Each man had a room to himself, and no one had an advantage. All rooms contained a shabby dresser with drawers that stuck, a sagging metal-framed bed, and walls with chipped and cracked paint. The communal bathroom for the floor was at the end of the hallway. After hastily unpacking, the men gathered and walked next door to the café that appeared to be no better than the hotel.

"Funny the desk clerk didn't know about us arriving," Jack said. "The only airplanes he knows about are some that land at the airport at the edge of town. Didn't he say they came and went from the west?"

"They must be the Western South American planes," the captain said. "They're supposed to get freight and mail and any passengers from us to head back across the Andes. And we're to take their mail and passengers north. In fact, we're supposed to meet with officials from the airline."

Ed shook his head. "Something's not right. Want to bet the phone number we have for Western is wrong?"

"I'll find out as soon as we finish eating," the captain said. "I'll try calling them."

"Yeah, something's up; I can feel it," Lyle said. "I was in a similar situation in Morocco, had a feeling things weren't as they should be. We barely got out with our lives. Bandits had set a trap for us, but we managed to get in the plane and off the ground before they got us."

The captain frowned. "So you think we may be in danger?"

Lyle shrugged. "We need to consider it."

After the meal, Ed made the taxi ride back to the docks and commandeered a boat to take food and water, as well as some hot coffee, to Harold. Then he rejoined the crew at the hotel and learned that, indeed, the phone number for Western South American Airways was invalid. The men were discussing what to do, when the hallway floorboards creaked under heavy footsteps, snapping the men to attention.

Wooden Planes

Over the early spring wheat fields of Kansas, the plane flew westward. The pilots guided the machine with six passengers in the cabin, the famous Notre Dame coach Knut Rockne among them. Rockne, like most of his fellow passengers, liked to fly for the ease and time savings it provided. Board the plane, sit back, read a newspaper, or look out the window and watch the landscape roll beneath the wings. This day, though, clouds began to obscure the view below.

Transcontinental and Western Air Flight 599 left Kansas City, Missouri, on the chilly morning of March 31, 1931, heading toward Wichita, Kansas, where it would take on fuel. Its final scheduled stop was Los Angeles, California. There, Rockne would participate in the filming of the movie *The Spirit of Notre Dame*.

Three 425 horsepower Pratt & Whitney radial engines pulled the Fokker F-10A through the air, a plane that consisted of thin wood veneer glued to a wooden framework.

The clouds grew denser and lower; fog and mist filled the air, and the plane flew lower, keeping the ground in sight. Nervous tension filled the cabin. Some passengers fidgeted, others turned back to their newspapers, only pretending to read, the words meaningless. Some looked straight ahead and others peered intently out the windows, catching glimpses of the ever-closer ground.

The wooden left wing sheared off with a cracking, snapping, ripping sound, and fluttered to the ground. The rest of the plane followed, impacting the earth half a mile later, a Kansas wheat field its final destination.

Chapter Eight

A man with a square jaw and piercing eyes stood in the doorway of the captain's room where the men had gathered. "You Williams?" he demanded.

"Yes. Who wants to know?"

"Randolph McClelland," the tall, broad-shoulder man replied. He wore his wavy, brown hair combed straight back.

"What do you want?"

The other men went on alert, ready to subdue the intruder if he made a move.

"I guess you know my history," McClelland said.

"I do," the captain replied. "I was flying for Caribbean Airways when the old man took over your operation."

"Took over! You mean stole it out from

under me!"

The men with the captain each took a step forward.

"But you know what?" McClelland continued. "He did me a favor in the long run. I've got more money now than I'd ever have had trying to run an airline."

"Oh?"

"Yeah, the mining business has been good to me."

"Then what do you want?"

"Actually, I'm here to give you fellas a heads-up. You expecting contact with Western South American?"

"Yeah, but we can't contact them. Got an invalid phone number."

"Go to the airport and meet the inbound plane," McClelland said. "Also, there'll be an agent there. Get the information from him."

The captain gave a single nod of acknowledgment. "Thanks."

"Be careful," McClelland urged. "Colombia and South American Airways has been busy recently. They've taken over some of Western's routes and have control of the one that comes here to Buenos Aires. They're using Western's livery on some of their planes, so don't be fooled. Just because it says WSAA on the side of the plane doesn't mean that's really who it is. You know Germany has been supporting CSAA for some time, and now they're moving in on Western's territory."

"How can they do that?"

"How'd Trapp get my airline? Strong-arm techniques. Don't think they won't try to muscle in on Caribbean Air's business too, by whatever means they can."

"Why would you care?" Ed asked. "Wouldn't you like to see Caribbean Air go under?"

"Sure I would. But I don't have anything against you fellas or any of the pilots and mechanics. It's Trapp I hate. I'm warning you fellas for your own safety. They may resort to sabotage, and that could be deadly. Or they could simply interfere with your plans, pay off officials here to keep Caribbean out of the area. They've done some of that already. Didn't have a dock for the plane, did you?"

"We didn't," Jack said. "Had to anchor it out in the harbor."

"They've paid off enough officials to hinder cooperation with you. Make it difficult for you to land here, and they'll step in and take over. Not a lot different from what Trapp did to me. Seems there's a couple of fellas doing the dirty work, a couple of Nazi Germans. They go by Alfred Holtz and Hans Frederick. Who knows if that's their real names."

"So there are two of them," Ed said. "They fly a single-engine plane?"

"Yeah, Messerschmitt 108. They're restricted to land of course, but they can get around quick in it. They've set up landing strips near some of the towns."

"We've seen the plane," Jack said. "It shows up once in a while and follows us. Like they're checking us over."

Ed's eyes narrowed. "I still don't understand why you're willing to help us. You really that concerned about our safety?"

"To be quite honest, it's not all altruistic. I've got personal reasons. I don't want the Nazis to take over because they'd get their hands on my mining business, and that'd cut into my profits. We can help each other; you keep your airline safe from them, and I'll keep my mining business."

"We'll try to make it work," the captain said. "Thank you for the information."

"Good luck." McClelland turned and walked out the door.

Lyle lit a Camel and asked, "Think he's on the up-and-up?"

The captain shrugged. "We'll find out. I need to get on the horn to Nassau, make my daily report. Jack, you come with me while I call."

The two pilots went downstairs to the desk to

use the phone while the rest of the crew settled into their rooms.

"Hello, Wilcox?" Captain Williams said into the phone. "We're getting along fine. Plane's working good, but we're having some problems here in Buenos Aires."

While Jack stood patiently by, Captain Williams explained the situation to Wilcox: the lack of facilities, the Adcock malfunction, and the apparent lack of interest on the part of the local officials. He didn't talk about the Germans or his encounter with McClelland—that information he'd discuss directly with the old man.

After he'd finished talking with Wilcox, he asked to be transferred to communications, then he handed the phone to Jack. "Here Jack. You can talk to Gail."

"Why?"

"What do you mean, why?"

Jack rolled his eyes and took the phone. "Hello. Hello, Vivian? Yes, I'm doing quite well. How are you? I thought Gail would be in for her shift. She isn't? Well, that's all right. I hope she gets to feeling better."

Jack listened while Vivian talked, bubbly and excited as usual. Then he said, "Thank you, Vivian. And tell Gail I'm sorry I missed her."

"What did Vivian say?" the captain asked as Jack

hung up. "Gail doing all right?"

"Yeah, she's fine. Now. Guess according to Vivian she was near hysterics when we were overdue at Recife. She's a worrier, you know. She was sick today, so Vivian's working over."

"She seems to have trouble with something stuffing up her head," Captain Williams said. "Gives her headaches, I guess."

Jack seemed to be in thought, far away. Finally he said, "It may not work with her, not if she's hysterical whenever I'm gone and out of touch."

"Huh?"

"Oh, I'm just thinking out loud, I guess. Just thinking if I date Gail, she's gonna worry whenever I'm gone, especially if I make any of these long-distance trips."

"I see."

"Yeah, I don't know, but I'll give it a try, you know, spend some time with her, get to know her better. She's a swell girl, you know."

"She is."

~

Next morning, Ed, Lyle, and Harold went to work checking out the plane, making sure all fasteners, cables, and controls were in perfect working order, and they carefully checked each engine, all done under Ed's supervision. In the meantime, Jack and Captain Williams caught a streetcar to the airport at the edge of town to await the Western South American Airways flight.

The streetcar wasn't like the sleek, aluminum cars of Rio de Janeiro, but the more common wooden cars with big windows, clunky in comparison. Electricity from overhead powerlines powered them, and they rolled along on a set of tracks down the middle of the street. The trip allowed them to see in more detail some of the sights they'd observed the evening before: statues, fountains, and markets. The car traveled down tree-lined boulevards, jacaranda and tipa trees growing from the ground that separated the street lanes. The petals of the jacaranda's purple flowers cover the ground in the springtime, giving the appearance of purple snow. The tipas' dark trunks and branches give the trees a burned appearance, a contrast to their yellow flowers. Though a warm, seventy-five-degree autumn day, winter was approaching in the southern hemisphere, and the tree blossoms were long gone, the trees beginning to shed leaves.

At one of the streetcar's stops, the men watched a man and a young boy with a cow and calf sell milk direct from the cow. A customer, a slender fellow with a white shirt, skinny black tie, and suspenders, drank the glass of fresh milk, paid the man with the cow, and then entered an office building. Man, boy, cow, and calf wandered on down the street to find the next customer.

People of various nationalities filled the streets. The women wore calf-length dresses, some flowing, others closer fitting, and hats—brim slouch hats and knit madcaps that could be stretched and shaped for each individual, as well as the latest: the angled beret. Most of the men wore suits and fedoras or straw hats, flat on top with flat brims. Though early in the day, a trio of street musicians played the accordion, guitar, and drum. People passed by on their way to conduct business; a few lingered to listen.

The markets were opening up. Vendors filled tables and bins beneath the white canvas canopies, and early morning shoppers looked over the wares. The bargaining and haggling began.

The streetcar passed the livestock arena. A massive white, wooden, red-roofed grandstand of seats and bleachers enclosed the arena where livestock shows were held. The shows were more than just showing off cows, horses, and sheep; they were also huge social events drawing crowds that filled the grandstand with people dressed in their finery. The place was already bustling with activity, men wrangling animals and preparing the grounds for the afternoon show.

After the long ride they got off at the airport, the end of the line, and walked to the terminal to wait on the inbound Western South American Airways plane.

WSAA used Fokker trimotor planes, a wood and fabric machine with a high wing and seating for a dozen passengers, a machine outdated by 1934. The heat and humidity of the coastal region played havoc with the wood and glue wing structure and, if not frequently maintained, would lead to structural failure. Wood and fabric were no longer allowed for commercial airplanes in the United States for this very reason, but in some areas of South America the planes still plied the skies, the dangers unknown to most passengers.

The plane that landed wasn't an ancient Fokker, but a new Junkers Ju-52, a trimotor airplane of corrugated metal construction with a steel tube framework beneath the surface. Also unlike the Fokker airplane, this was a low-wing design and carried seventeen passengers. Though the plane said WSAA on its sides, the men had their doubts. When they walked out onto the apron and met the crew, the German accents as well as the uniforms confirmed suspicions. Unlike the special uniforms the Caribbean Airways men wore, the Germans, as was the norm with most airlines, wore military-influenced uniforms. The men wore gray pants, light blue shirts, and gray military officers' caps devoid of insignia. Though the men wore their shirts buttoned all the way up, they wore no neckties.

The German pilots were cordial, though reserved, evasive in their responses to questions.

"How long have you had the Junkers?" the captain asked.

"Not long," the German captain replied.

The copilot agreed. "*Ja*, not much time."

"What about the Fokker trimotors?" Jack asked. "I thought that's what Western South American Airlines used."

"*Ja*, we did," replied the German captain. "But we have new Junkers. A much better plane."

Jack nodded. "It looks like a nice plane."

The German captain gave a slight smile. "Come aboard. See how nice it is."

The four men boarded the plane, now devoid of passengers and freight. The Germans pointed out the cabin with its comfortable seats, and then they directed the Americans to the cockpit and had Captain Williams and Jack take the pilot seats.

"You're missing a throttle." Jack pointed to the three throttle levers on the center console.

The German men looked at each other, puzzled, then broke out in laughter. "*Nein*, not missing," said the copilot. "One extra!"

"No, our plane has four engines," Jack said.

"Four?"

"Four. Four of them at 750 horsepower each and variable-pitch propellers. It cruises at 150 miles per hour too."

"Are you joking with us?" the copilot asked. "Some American humor?"

"No, sir, no joke."

"Well, then, that is some airplane."

"You will be getting passengers, mail, and freight from us," the captain explained, turning the conversation toward business. "We'll have a truck bring it from the docks to the airfield here."

"I know nothing about that," the German captain said.

"You know nothing about Caribbean Airways coming down the east coast of the continent?"

The German captain shook his head. "*Nein*. And I know nothing of any kind of agreement to receive passengers and freight from such an airline."

The men exited the German machine and continued their conversation outside.

Captain Williams addressed the German captain. "Do you know of Colombia and South American Airways?"

The two Germans conversed in their own language, then the captain asked, "Colombia and

South American?"

"Yes," the captain said.

"Maybe. Up north there is an airline; they fly airplanes on floats. We have heard of them."

"They don't operate this far south?" asked Jack.

"*Nein, nein*, not this far."

Jack and the captain looked at each other, then the captain asked, "Do you know Alfred Holtz?"

"A pilot with us?"

"A pilot, but I don't know if he flies for the airline."

"Holtz?" the German captain asked the copilot. Again, the men conversed in German, then the captain said, "*Nein*, no Holtz."

"Are you fellas overnighting here?" the captain asked.

"*Nein*," the copilot replied. "We head back in about one hour to Santiago."

"Have a safe flight," the captain said.

"You men also," the German captain responded.

Jack and the captain entered the terminal and talked with the WSAA agent. Though having no awareness of the freight and passenger agreement with Caribbean Airways, he was helpful, giving the men the phone number for the main office. Unlike the two pilots, he wasn't German.

After business with the agent, the two men caught the streetcar back into town, got off near the dockyard, and went in search for an office of anyone who was in charge of overseeing the docks. They dodged around the Model T trucks, horse-drawn carts, and people hurrying on foot and on bicycle. At the far end, away from the chaos, they eventually found the dock for oceangoing passenger ships. A ship was unloading passengers.

Jack and the captain entered the passenger line terminal and were directed to the manager's office. The manager was little help and made it clear he wasn't interested in airline business for it would most likely take away from ocean liner business. The men did at least learn who in the city government was in charge of transportation.

Jack and Captain Williams navigated their way back through the busy docks. They caught a glimpse of Holtz milling about in and out of the crowds and ducking behind trucks and carts. They shadowed him and saw him meet another man behind a parked truck. The two talked, constantly looking around, and when they spotted Jack and the captain, they each took off in separate directions.

The captain shook his head. "Might as well let them go."

Downtown at the government office, the two men met Silvio Rossi, the director of city transportation. A clean-shaven man, of Italian descent, Rossi was a slender man with dark hair pomaded and combed back. He wore a dark blue pin-striped suit and red necktie—a dapper looking fellow.

"Mr. Rossi," the captain said, "we represent Caribbean Airways and are the pilots of the plane in the harbor."

"Yes, what can I help you with?"

"There should have been docking facilities and fuel storage in place here, but we found none. Also, our Adcock radio navigation station was shut off."

"I'm not aware of any of this."

"Did you not talk with John Trapp in New York City, the president of Caribbean Airways?"

"Hmmm." He rubbed his chin, appearing deep in thought. "Trapp? No, I don't think so."

"Would he have talked with anyone else from this office?"

"If he had, I'd know. The information would've been passed onto me. I know of everything that goes on here."

"I'm sure you do," Jack said. "There must be a mix-up of some sort. Caribbean Airways has the mail contract as far south as Buenos Aires, so we'll be your only source for international mail."

"What are you implying?"

"I'm not implying anything. I'm stating that we have the mail contract, and it's the only way it'll be delivered here. So facilities need to be in place."

Captain Williams nodded. "That's right. We'll begin scheduled service in a month, and we expect a dock for us. Also, a passenger terminal will eventually be needed. John Trapp will be in contact with you once again."

"Good day, gentlemen," Rossi said, signaling he was done with the conversation. "Oh, one thing. You owe the city for anchoring your plane in the harbor."

"Take that up with Trapp," the captain said.

~

The men gathered for the evening meal. This time they walked several blocks to a finer establishment than the one next to the hotel. They discussed the events of the day. Jack and the captain related their trying experiences, and Ed, who had good news, declared the plane fit for flight, but there was one major problem—fuel. They'd have to have fuel transported from the airfield west of the city to the harbor, and then out to the plane.

After the meal, Ed wandered off, as usual, on some secret mission to ferret out further deals, and Lyle also vanished into the humid night. Harold caught a boat to the plane, where he'd guard it for the night, and Jack and Captain Williams sat in the lobby, watching the handful of people coming and going. Unlike the clientele of the hotel in Rio—well-dressed people who had children with them—the people at this hotel appeared to be on the seedy side. Slick-looking men and painted women strolled back and forth, and in and out of the lobby, and up and down the creaky stairs.

"Jack," the captain said suddenly, "I've been thinking about giving up the chief pilot position. When Jennifer and I get married, I want more home time. Right now, it seems I'm married to this job."

After a stunned pause, Jack asked, "Giving up the chief pilot job? Are you serious?"

"Deadly serious."

"So you and Jennifer are getting married soon?"

"Yes, I'm ready, and I know she is."

"Going to set a date when we get back?"

"Yeah, it's one of the first things I want to do."

"But you'll still fly, won't you?" Jack asked. "If you give up the chief pilot job."

"Yes, I'll still fly, but I just want to be a line pilot, have a schedule. That way Jennifer and I can plan things, and she can expect me home at a certain time. Also, I think the old man is looking at buying Pacific Airways. They got the second S-42 off the line from Sikorsky, and they plan to expand out across the Pacific. Right now they're just serving the west coast, but that's about to change. I'm afraid if I don't give up my position, I'll be expected to do survey flights out there. I don't want that."

After a pause in the conversation, Jack speculated, "Wonder how Harold is doing."

"He's no doubt enjoying the peace and quiet," the captain said.

"He's working out all right, but I had my doubts at first."

"I think he just got off on the wrong foot. He was a bit standoffish, but I think he just wasn't comfortable. He's pretty tight-lipped about his personal life. I wonder sometimes if he had a bad experience along the way somewhere."

"Could be. Maybe in the military. Seems he'd have trouble fitting in. Maybe a woman did him wrong. Remember the conversation when we were talking about women? Remember Harold said something like good women are scarce, and if you find one who likes you, hang on to her?"

"I do remember, now that you mention it."

"That could be why he's the way he is. Or it could be something else. Who knows? Anyway, he seems to be adjusting. Still can't believe he's never flown before taking this job. At least he's more relaxed now."

"Yeah, he's adjusting. He does know his radios. I've got complete confidence in him. And he volunteered to spend another night in the plane."

"I'm guessing he likes the solitude."

"I'm guessing you're right."

~

Out in the darkened harbor, the plane gently rocked at anchor. Harold rested on the floor in the cabin, stretched out on some blankets, dozing off to sleep. The sounds of dockyard activity had become normal: the muffled rumble of trucks, the voices of men shouting orders, the mechanical creaking and groaning of cranes and hoists loading cargo onto the ships. In the background of the dock noise was the deep chugging sound of the ships themselves as they moved in and out of the harbor to receive loads of goods before heading out to distant lands. These rhythmic sounds lulled Harold off into that gray zone when reality begins to fade and dreams take over. A steady tap, tap, tap filled his senses. He began to slip into deeper slumber. A steady tap, tap, tap from somewhere above. The gentle rocking of the plane was soothing, lulling, sleep and dreams spreading deeper.

Harold suddenly sat bolt upright. He listened. The soft tap, tap, tap was definitely real—footsteps across the top of the fuselage, heading toward the trailing edge of the wing. Harold ran to the back of the plane, flashlight in hand, and rummaged through the spare parts and tools. He found a sturdy three-foot piece of pipe and raced forward to the flight deck. With the flashlight turned off, he quietly eased open the crew hatch and climbed atop the forward fuselage. In the dim lighting, he saw a man kneeling on the number three engine nacelle.

He aimed the flashlight, turned it on, and yelled, "Hey! Whaddaya think you're doing?"

The man leaped to his feet, ran to the trailing edge of the wing, jumped down onto the fuselage, and then slid down into a waiting boat. The boat operator started the engine, and the men sped away across the darkened harbor.

~

Ed wandered into the lobby, perpetual cigar clamped in his teeth and a paper bag under his left arm.

"Hey, Butz!" Jack called out.

Ed turned and saw the two men sitting in the overstuffed chairs with armrests worn threadbare. "Hey, fellas," Ed responded as he approached them. He set the bag down, pulled up a third chair, and collapsed into it.

"Ed, you seem tired," the captain said.

"I am. It was a long day checking over the plane, and I've had a bit of a trying evening, though it was successful."

"What'd you get, Ed?"

"I got fuel lined up. They have plenty at the airfield, and I negotiated for enough to fill our tanks. They'll bring it over by truck in the morning, then we have to pump it into a tank on a boat and take it out to the plane. A time-consuming process."

"What else you got?" Captain Williams asked.

"Here in the bag, I've got some cherry vanilla pipe tobacco for Harold and a dozen good cigars for myself. Sure you fellas don't want to try one?"

Jack shook his head. "We're sure."

"Also learned a little more about our German friends. They're definitely helping CSAA, and their plan is to stop us by any means, so we can't fulfill our mail contract. Then they'll step in and take over."

Jack frowned. "Interesting. We met a couple of pilots who said they were with WSAA, but they were Germans, and they were flying a new Junkers. The plane had WSAA painted on the side, but it looked like a hasty job, pretty sloppy."

"Wonder how they took Western's flight. Suppose the one that comes here from Santiago is the only one they have?"

"Maybe you can find out."

"On an unrelated topic, I discovered a classy hotel, the Plaza Hotel—first-class, seven or eight stories high. Next time we come this way, we'll stay there. Be a good place for our passengers too. And another, unrelated topic: I've been studying the fuel dumps on the plane. Something's not right there; they're just not designed quite right. I can't figure out what, but something's wrong with them."

"What do you mean?" the captain asked.

"Well, where the fuel dumps overboard. The way they're located doesn't seem right."

"What trouble could it cause?"

"I think the fuel would be affected by the air flowing off the wing. It may be nothing; it may flow right on out behind the wing, but if it's somehow pulled back inside and toward the engines, there could be a problem. A serious problem."

"Wouldn't you think the Sikorsky engineers would have that figured out?" Jack asked.

"They should. They probably do, but it just seems kinda odd to me the way it's configured. I do want to get with the fellas at Sikorsky after we get back and go over it. Something just bothers me about the way it's designed."

Early in the morning, just as he was about to go meet the other crew members for breakfast, someone knocked at Jack's door. He opened it to face a stranger, a tall, thin fellow dressed in a light-colored suit, holding a matching hat in his hands.

"Captain Williams?" the man asked.

"No, sir, I'm Jack Smith, the copilot. Captain Williams is out."

"Maybe you can help me. I'm from the city, the office of transportation. You can't tell anyone I was here; I could get into big trouble, even lose my job."

Jack listened intently.

"May I come in so we can talk privately?"

"Certainly." Jack closed the door after the man entered the room. "You must have something quite important to say."

"I feel I do. It's about your facilities here, or rather your lack of." The man paused, looking at the hat he was turning over in his hands.

"Yes, go on," Jack urged.

"Well, you see, my boss, the minister of transportation, received money to stall the project. You know, the project to build a dock for you and have a fuel supply. Corruption, it's prolific here."

"And you want money for your information?"

"No! No, I just want to do what's right. You see, not all of us are bad. It's only certain people, and that makes it bad on the rest of us."

"Is the mayor being bribed?"

"I don't think so. He seems to want to run an honest government. But he doesn't know everything that goes on. I was in a meeting when he expressed his excitement about your airline coming to Buenos Aires, all the potential for freight and visitors it would bring as well as the mail. He doesn't want Colombia and South American Airlines to get a foothold here. He wants to keep Nazis out of the city."

"I hope he's successful. Seems they want to get a grip on things here."

"Yes, I believe they do, and they're evil; they hate certain kinds of people. I'm one of them, being Jewish. It concerns me what they may do in Europe, and if we don't stop them, what they'll do here. I've been hearing things, and I'm afraid some of it is true."

Jack sighed. "Yes, the world situation doesn't look good. This depression, I'm afraid, has opened the door to these crazy people. They'll promise what the people want, and they'll get into power, and then show their true colors."

"Hitler's doing that now. He's going to doom his own country, but the people can't see that; they just listen to his useless promises, and they're swayed by his rhetoric." After a pause, the man said, "I'll get you in to see the mayor. I'll call and leave a message at the desk here at the hotel when I get a time verified."

"Can you do it today? We plan to leave early tomorrow morning."

"I'm confident I can."

~

On their way back from breakfast, the desk clerk stopped the men and gave them the message promised by the man from the transportation office. The mayor would see them at ten o'clock. Jack and the captain would make the meeting while the rest of the crew waited. Ed went to the plane to relieve Harold, who took the opportunity to clean up and eat. Lyle spent time going over the charts, plotting the course northward, and estimating flying time, arrival times, and compass headings. He called the maritime station for weather reports and wind forecasts, and then figured the forecasts into his estimates.

Jack and Captain Williams returned by noon and joined the other two men for lunch.

"Well, what did you find out?" Harold asked.

"The mayor was oblivious to our needs or even to our arriving here," the captain replied. "He kept waiting to hear from us about details on facilities. Seems the transportation minister withheld all that from him, and he wasn't too happy. He's aware of the

Nazi influence and wants to put a halt to it. He said he'll do everything in his power to assist Caribbean Airways and make sure Colombia and South American doesn't get a foothold. The mail contract is our insurance, and he knows that. Before we left, he was on the phone to get things moving on a dock and fuel storage. He said he'd call the old man as soon as we left and work out details with him."

After lunch, Harold took the boat ride to the plane to relieve Ed so he could eat. The boat operator was thrilled to see him. The flight crew had proven good for his business as they shuttled back and forth several times daily. Upon arriving, Harold found Ed, clad in his greasy coveralls, on the work platform for number four engine, his arms deep into the engine, his cigar, unlit for safety reasons, clamped between his teeth. He looked up at the sound of footsteps.

"'Bout time you got here," he growled.

"Well, wrap it up there and get going," Harold said.

"I'll be right down."

Ed was navigating his way through the busy dockyard, dodging the trucks, carts, and clusters of people, when a voice yelled out, "Hey, when you gonna move that airplane?" He turned to face a tall, burly man with three-day-old stubble on his face and curly brown hair in disarray.

"When we're ready." Ed clamped down tighter on his cigar, which was now lit.

"Well, you better get ready real soon."

"You better get used to seeing a plane here, fella. We'll be flying in on a regular basis soon."

"We don't want no airplanes cluttering up the harbor. We got work to do here."

Ed stood his ground, though the dockhand was half a foot taller. The men stared at each other, and finally the man said, "I don't got no time to bother with you." He turned abruptly and walked off.

Fireside Chat

It was time. In the cities and in the remote rural regions of the country, radios were turned on and tuned in, and amid the static and crackling and popping came a voice, authoritative, clear, distinctive. Though the voice sounded strange to the midwesterners and the southerners, certain words pronounced oddly, they revered the definite northeastern accent. In the households, even the children paused at its sound. Adults hung on each word, clinging to them as if clinging to life preservers. The man behind the voice may even save their lives, maybe not directly, but through his actions and programs designed to help pull the people out of the desperate situation they were in. Promises were made to get help to people, provide them with work, restore their dignity, give them hope for a bright future that seemed so far away it couldn't be true, for it had been dark far too long.

The voice filled the room, comforting the hurting and discouraged. Even the children, though not fully understanding, knew something special was happening. It was a New Deal. It promised new life. It promised hope. Franklin Delano Roosevelt, who took office March 4, 1933, chatted with people across the country through the radio waves. Maybe he wasn't at the fireside in the homes in person, but he was there in spirit, through his voice.

Chapter Nine

At dawn, the men prepared for takeoff. Fuel had been delivered late the day before, being trucked over from the airfield and then pumped into drums on a boat, from where it was subsequently pumped into the airplane's fuel tanks. Ed carefully drained samples from the tanks to check for any water or other contaminants that would've settled to the bottom overnight. It checked out fine, much to everyone's relief.

Though the weather forecast called for some potentially heavy storms along the route, the sky dawned clear, the sun bright orange as it climbed above the horizon. A small crowd of spectators slowly gathered at the passenger terminal dock as word spread that the mysterious, four-engine airplane that had been floating in the harbor was going to be lifting off. After making the preflight checks, the crew was ready to start the engines. The propeller on number one engine jerked to life and rotated hesitantly; smoke puffed out the exhaust stacks, then, with a bang followed by a flash of flame, the engine came to life. Once it settled into an easy idle, the process was repeated for each engine until all four were settled into the easy, loping idle, and the big propellers turned lazily. The people on shore—some with sleepy-eyed children clinging to parents' legs—watched intently, voices muffled as they speculated as to what would come next.

Ed made his way into the plane's bow and retrieved the anchor, and the plane moved forward from the pull of the four slow-turning propellers. After stowing the anchor, he hurried back to his station to monitor engine life, fuel flow, and fuel and oil pressure. The pilots eased out of the harbor, threading their way around ships and the motorboats that zipped around, and headed for open water for takeoff.

The spectators strained to watch, the view occasionally blocked by ships before the plane disappeared totally behind a large freighter, the sound of its engines disappearing with it. The people waited, their voices rising as they tried to understand where the plane had gone. Some began to head for home.

Suddenly, the long wings of the plane blocked the early morning sun from view as it roared overhead, the engines at full power, propellers at high RPM, sending vibrations through the bodies of everyone on the dock. Even the dockhands turned to look up. Then it was gone, as if the sky had swallowed it up, and all that could be heard was, once again, the familiar noise of the dockyard. The people slowly made their way home to morning chores. Life resumed its routine.

Inside the plane, Jack held the control wheel firmly. His left hand reached overhead to the throttles and propeller controls, while his feet moved in coordination with left and right control wheel movements. He eased the plane up into a climb and made a sweeping turn to put them on course for Rio de Janeiro.

They followed a straight path which would take them over the jungle of Uruguay and then into Brazil for several hundred miles before crossing open water. About an hour into the flight, clouds appeared in the northwest, not puffy cumulus but towering cumulonimbus with tops that boiled into the upper reaches of the atmosphere. Ahead of this, a wall of dark clouds advanced rapidly, bringing winds that burst out with the strength to bend trees in the jungle.

The blackness grew, growing across the length of the horizon, encroaching and surrounding the speeding plane and quickly cutting off any avenue of escape.

"Captain," Jack said, "that gust front is awful strong. I think we need to divert course."

"I've been watching." The captain studied the blackening sky with a steady gaze. "Let's head back to Buenos Aires. It's our only safe option. We can't get around it and can't get over the top." He announced his intentions to the rest of the crew and had Harold contact the maritime station in Buenos Aires to inform them of their intentions and to check the weather.

A few minutes later, Harold responded. "Captain, the storm's approaching Buenos Aires. It'll hit before we can arrive."

"I can see the clouds now, just over the horizon," Jack said. "Captain, we're surrounded."

The sky all around them had turned dark with a green tint, the black clouds boiling. There was no escape. They climbed to get as much altitude as they could, Jack having turned the plane eastward toward the ocean. At fourteen thousand feet they met the storm.

"Hang on!" the captain said. "It's gonna be a wild ride."

Each man pulled his seat belt as tight as it could

go. Harold grabbed the edge of his table, holding on with both hands. Lyle had stowed his charts, pencils, and plotters. The captain took the controls, and Jack held them lightly, ready to assist if needed. Ed clamped down on his cigar and made a last-minute check of the gauges because once the plane was slammed around, they'd be unreadable.

The plane seemed to plunge into night, and the rain hammered the fuselage so hard the men couldn't even hear the engines. The turbulence batted the plane up and down, the pilots letting the altitude vary rather than take a chance on overstressing the airframe. All they were concerned about was keeping the wings relatively level so they didn't go inverted.

The pilots depended on the flight instruments to control the plane since the outside world was in total darkness. The instruments became difficult to read, blurred, the needles shaking and dancing from the turbulence. All the men could do was estimate the attitude of the airplane, but it was enough for them to keep upright and maintain the necessary amount of control.

Then the hail began.

It pounded against the plane, hammered into the aluminum, and beat on the windscreen. A blinding flash of lightning left the men stunned, then a softball-size chunk of hail smashed against the windscreen, punching a gaping hole on the captain's side. He held up his hands to shield his face. The ice projectile missed the captain and crashed against the bulkhead at the rear of the flight deck, shattering into hundreds of pieces. Though the pilots had slowed the plane for the turbulence, the hundred-mile-per-hour wind blasted through the jagged opening, sweeping in buckets of rain.

The sound of the roaring wind filled the cockpit. The men couldn't yell loud enough to be heard even through the intercom. Jack took command of the controls and slowed the plane even more. Ed and Harold helped the captain out of his seat, and Lyle scurried onto the flight deck to investigate the racket. He immediately lent a hand. The captain, shouting but not being heard, waved the men away. He was drenched; his hat was lost, and his hair fell into his eyes.

Ed resumed his station and monitored engine function, afraid the driving rain would find its way into the engines. Though he couldn't make out the gauges in detail, he could see temperatures had cooled, though still in the safe zone, but engine speed was slowing on number one and two. He switched on the carburetor heat to melt any ice that may have built up in the venturis, and the engines dropped more RPM.

Though not directly in line of the blast of air coming through the damaged windscreen, wind and rain blew on Ed and on his gauges. His cigar was soggy and had gone out, but still he kept it clamped in his mouth. He signaled the captain that they needed to land as soon as possible. The captain went to the cabin with Lyle, where the noise was muffled enough they could talk. Lyle pulled out his charts, spread them out on the bucking table, and searched for the closest water for a landing. The floor dropped out from under him and the captain as the plane hit a violent downdraft. They grabbed ahold of the navigation table to steady themselves. Lyle pointed to Porto Alegre, a city near the coast on an inlet on the northern edge of Lagoa dos Patos, a large lake. It was one hundred miles to the east, requiring over an hour's worth of flying time at their reduced speed. With luck, though, they'd break through and get ahead of the storm and touch down in clear weather.

Captain Williams went back to the flight deck with the new compass heading and destination information written on a piece of paper to give to Jack. Though struggling to read the compass, Jack turned to the new heading, then he pointed to number one engine, which was barely visible through the pouring rain. The propeller had stopped. He looked at Ed, who was battling wind and rain at his station but still monitored and worked engine controls. The captain turned and headed back to the cabin.

He went to the rear of the plane, bouncing side to side, grabbing onto anything he could as he went. Once there he dug through the tools and supplies stashed in the cargo area. After rummaging around, he pulled out a piece of plywood and some rope, then he fought his way forward, struggling with the plywood, and explained to Lyle what he had in mind. The two of them went to the flight deck where Harold was now kneeling beside Jack, helping him read gauges, using hand signals to communicate. His perpetual pipe was still lit and clamped tightly between his teeth.

The pilot's seat offered some protection to Ed, as it deflected the wind and rain, which had not eased up; nevertheless Ed was drenched, and his cigar, having lost the battle, was nowhere to be seen. The captain and Lyle wrestled the plywood across the back of the pilot's seat, and as Lyle held it in place, the captain lashed it tightly with the rope. This offered more protection for Ed.

Darkness still shrouded the plane, the clouds so dense and the rain so intense that the wingtips were invisible. The men were only able to see just beyond the outboard engines. Jack worked the controls, wheel, and rudder pedals, his eyes in constant motion scanning the flight instruments as he fought to maintain control. Harold, still kneeling beside Jack's seat, clung to anything he could find. In order to assist Jack, he signaled gain and loss of altitude, left and right attitude, and airspeed increasing or decreasing. Between the two of them, the plane remained in a relatively stable attitude.

Eventually, the rain slackened, the clouds lightened, and the wingtips became visible again. The men were able to talk to each other if they got close and yelled, for tremendous wind noise still screamed in through the flight deck, making intercom communications useless. The propeller on number one engine began to turn as Ed attempted a restart. Smoke blew back in the slipstream, then the engine roared to life, and Ed made adjustments. Harold returned to his station, and the captain took his place kneeling beside Jack. Lyle followed their progress on the chart, plotted time remaining, and determined the point for descent.

When the time came, Lyle stepped onto the flight deck and signaled Jack it was time to begin descent. Jack throttled back the engines, and the plane eased down through the clouds. Jack and Captain Williams both scanned the flight gauges. Harold tuned the frequency for the maritime station, though communication would prove difficult, if not impossible, with the wind noise. As they descended, the clouds lightened more, the rain stopped, and they burst into bright sunshine. The storm behind them, though, followed quickly. They had to land before it reached them. A landing in such turbulence and low visibility would be deadly. Jack eased the nose down a bit more to hurry the descent.

He leveled off at twenty-five hundred feet. The lush green landscape rolled by beneath the wings, and soon the lake came into sight over the nose, just as Lyle had predicted. Jack slowed the plane to eighty miles per hour, the wind sound decreasing accordingly. He would overfly the lake first to check for obstructions and boat traffic, then circle back to land. As he turned southward, the men could see the storm front approaching from the west, the wall of black clouds barreling down on them. There would be only one chance to land and anchor.

Jack circled and approached again, this time lowering the flaps and slowing to landing speed. The captain, unable to use his seat, remained kneeling on the floor and held firmly to the back of Jack's seat to brace for the landing. The plane slowed more; the water rose up to meet them, and then with a thud, the plane touched down. As it slowed, the wind noise through the damaged windscreen subsided, finally fading out totally. Jack quickly taxied toward an inlet that would provide some protection from the storm. At his command, Ed, who'd made his way to the bow, lowered the anchor. In the meantime, the captain had taken Ed's station and coordinated with Jack to shut down the engines. Then the storm hit.

"We gotta go through this again?" Harold yelled.

Lyle entered the flight deck. "At least we're not in the air this time."

The plane shook and rocked, then the rain pounded with a deafening sound against the aluminum fuselage. The men silently rode out the storm. Lyle, the only one standing, clung to the copilot's seat back. After what seemed an eternity, but actually was only ten minutes, the rain let up, and the clouds gradually began to lift.

"Let's get to work," Ed said as he entered the flight deck from the bow where he had ridden out the storm. "I think we can fasten this piece of plywood to the outside of the window frame."

He and the captain unlashed the sheet of plywood from the seat back and maneuvered it outside through the hatch and onto the forward fuselage. They made a trial fit. It would easily cover the opening. Ed went to the cargo compartment and dug out some tools and supplies. When he returned, the captain held the plywood in position, and Ed used a hand-operated drill to make pilot holes in the wood and windscreen frame. He then secured the plywood with sheet-metal screws.

"It should hold," Ed announced. "Maybe we should keep the speed down a bit, though."

In the meantime, Harold and Lyle went to the rear of the plane and out through the passenger entrance. They stood on top of the fuselage, stretching and breathing in fresh air. Lyle lit a Camel, and Harold, after carefully packing his pipe, lit it.

Having secured the plywood, Ed and the two pilots made an inspection for hail damage. The metal fuselage was strong and had held up well with only a few small dents. The leading edges of the wings, though, were a bit more damaged with several major dents. The control surfaces, which were fabric covering a steel framework, had fared well except for the portside aileron. Fabric hung shredded from a couple of areas the hail had punctured.

"What do you make of that, Ed?" Jack asked. "Can you repair it?"

"No, I don't have any fabric or glue, but I think we can make do."

The captain looked at him. "What do you mean?"

"The main thing is to keep the fabric from tearing any more. I'll trim the loose fabric back to the nearest rib. There'll still be holes, of course, but without the torn ends flappin' in the wind, the damage may not go any further."

Ed pulled out his pocketknife and carefully cut away loose and damaged material. After putting away tools and supplies, the men were ready to continue the trek northward. Captain Williams relieved Jack of flying duties. He took the copilot's seat since the pilot's seat was unusable. Jack knelt beside the captain to assist with takeoff, calling out airspeed and helping to check flight gauges. Once airborne, he went back to the cabin to stretch out and relax; he was physically and mentally exhausted. The men had clear skies for the remainder of the flight to Rio, the storm having passed well to the east.

It was nearly dark by the time they touched down. They tied up at the dock that had been built just for them and, as on the trip south, a couple of police officers met the men and stood guard over the plane. For this the men were thankful, for they wanted nothing more than a good meal and a good night's sleep. Even Ed stayed in for the night.

Captain Williams made a call to Nassau to apprise them of the ordeal and let them know they were safely in Rio but would be delayed at least a day for repairs.

Next morning, the men took a thorough look at the plane, inspecting closely for damage they may have missed under the tenuous conditions on the lake. Ed determined that the dents in the leading edge, while interfering somewhat with airflow, posed no major problem. The torn fabric on the aileron was a different story—it had to be fixed, as did the windscreen. He ventured off to find supplies. While Ed was gone, the other four men went over the plane in detail. They'd learned from Ed what to look for, what was acceptable, and what wasn't. Though they couldn't make repairs themselves, they'd note discrepancies for Ed to examine.

As the men worked, they were somewhat surprised at the sound of another airplane flying overhead. They looked up to see a single-engine machine with retractable landing gear zipping by. It appeared to be the Messerschmitt 108. It made only the one high-speed pass and disappeared inland beyond the city.

Ed returned by noon with fabric and glue to repair the damaged aileron. A fella in a truck delivered a piece of Triplex Safety Glass cut precisely to replace the shattered windscreen, and he stayed to assist in installation. All afternoon, the men crawled over the outside of the plane, walking over the wings and fuselage, resembling a bunch of ants on a piece of food. By evening, all was finished, the plane buttoned up, and the police guards in place.

While they were relaxing at the hotel, the desk summoned Captain Williams to let him know he had a phone call. The call came from the dock. The police officers on guard had tangled with a man who'd attempted to sneak onto the plane. He'd gotten away and disappeared into the crowd, but the officers described him as having dark hair, parted in the middle, and being clean-shaven. Not Holtz, the usual suspect.

That night after dinner, the men split up as usual, Ed venturing off by himself and Lyle doing the same. Harold, though, joined Jack and the captain for a stroll through the streets rather than staying by himself.

Ed headed toward the docks, not where the airplane was tied up, but off to the far end among the warehouses. He met a couple of fellows in the shadows and offered them cigarettes. The match to light them illuminated the area, casting long shadows on the warehouse wall beside which they stood.

Ed puffed on his perpetual cigar. "So what can you fellas tell me?"

"What do you want to know?" asked the taller, thinner one.

"That plane that flew over today. Was that the German machine?"

"German?" asked the shorter man, slightly portly in build. He wore a dark hat pulled low on his forehead.

"German."

The man turned to his friend and discussed in Portuguese, gesturing with his hands. Then he turned back to Ed and said, "Yeah, German."

"How many men?"

"Two."

"What do they want?"

Again, the two men conversed in their native language, then the portly man said, "We don't know what they want."

Ed puffed on his cigar, then said, with cigar clamped in the corner of his mouth, "I don't buy that. I know you fellas have connections."

"Connections, yes, but we don't know everything."

"Two cartons of Camels and I won't turn you in to the police says you do know everything."

The two men looked at each other, then the taller one said, "They want to stop your airline."

"We figured that much. How?"

"Any way they can. They'll do damage to your plane and harm you if they have to."

"Where do these men stay?"

"That we don't know. They're in and out. They seem to just vanish."

"It's true," the portly man said. "We don't know exactly where they stay. But they have to land at the airstrip at the edge of town. There's a landing strip at the edge of the jungle west of the city. We've not been there, but we know of it. That has to be where they come and go. Maybe they have a hut to sleep in. We don't know. You do know the city officially doesn't want them here. The police have done their best to keep them away, but there are a few within the government who are working with them, with the Germans."

"Thanks, fellas." Ed reached into his bag and produced the promised cartons of cigarettes. "Now, can you direct me to a source of engine parts? In particular, Pratt & Whitney engine parts."

Meanwhile, Lyle was in a back-alley craps game and losing badly. He'd returned to the Lapa neighborhood, lured there by the call of drink and women, as usual, and in addition this time, gambling. He began to realize why he didn't gamble much as each roll of the dice took his money. He cut his losses while he still had enough left for drink and made a straight line to the nearest tavern, which was conveniently placed below a second-floor massage parlor. He ordered a shot of whiskey at the bar, tossed it down, and lit a Camel. He ordered another shot. A woman sat down next to him and mentioned she was thirsty. Lyle ordered an overpriced drink for her. She thanked him and began to chat, small talk, then suggestive talk, then the two of them exited the bar and entered the door a few feet down the sidewalk that led to the upstairs.

When Lyle left the building, a man stepped from the shadows, blocking his path.

Lyle tried to step around the man. "Excuse me."

The stranger sidestepped to block Lyle.

Lyle frowned. "Hey, what's wrong with you?"

The man was about the same height as Lyle, slender, though not skinny, dressed in a dark suit with no tie, and wearing a hat.

"It's you who's gonna have the problem," the man said in a slight accent, American or European.

"I don't think so!" Lyle didn't back away; he faced the man squarely.

The man reached inside his jacket, and Lyle took that opportunity to throw a punch. Something, paper, or a photo, fell from the man's hand as he reeled backward. Lyle stepped forward and threw another punch, which the stranger managed to slip. Lyle took a quick glance around and saw a few people on the street, though they paid no attention to the altercation.

The man, whose hat had fallen off, readied another punch. Lyle took a step back but caught a shoe on a buckled spot in the sidewalk and stumbled. His arms flailed as he tried to catch himself. The stranger was about to unload his punch when another man grabbed him from behind and flung him to the ground.

"Ed! Glad to see you!" Lyle scurried to get up and help hold the man down.

Ed grinned. "Well, I was just in the neighborhood."

"This neighborhood?"

"Yeah, because I knew I'd find you here. Wanted to keep you out of trouble and looks like I got here just in time." Ed turned his attention to the man pinned to the ground. "Who are you?"

The man made no reply.

"I'll ask you one more time, then I'll quit bein' nice. Who are you?"

"John Smith. I'm American."

"I don't think so," Ed said. "I don't know any Smith with an accent like that. I'd guess you're German. Lyle, check him for some identification."

Lyle reached inside the man's jacket and pulled out a wallet containing money and photos, the pictures taken in downtown Berlin. "You're correct, Ed. German, got to be."

"You one of the fellas dogging us?" Ed asked.

"Dogging?"

"Following. You know, keeping track of us."

The man didn't respond.

"Lyle," Ed said, "you know the local authorities don't want Nazis hangin' around. I think we should turn him over to the police."

"I think you're correct, Mister Butz."

"I'll keep this fella down, you go in the pub and make a phone call."

As Lyle got up, the man said, "No! I'll tell you what you want. No police."

Ed nodded. "All right. What are you doing here?"

"You're right; I'm tracking you, observing what you do. But I'm not a Nazi. I have Brazilian citizenship."

"Those photos were taken in Berlin," Lyle said. "I recognize the buildings."

"Yes, they were taken there. Those are my parents with me in the picture. I was home visiting."

"Why are you watching us?" Ed asked. "Is that your single-engine plane that we keep seein'?"

"I don't know how to fly. Did you find a pilot license in my wallet?"

Ed looked at Lyle, who said, "No, I guess not."

"Is your name Hans?" Ed asked. "Hans Frederick?"

"No." The man turned to Lyle and asked, "Didn't you read my identification you took from me? Look at my name."

Lyle opened the wallet and looked again. In the dim light, he read the name. "This says his name is Erich Heinrichs.

"Is the name Heinrichs familiar?" The man

directed his question to Lyle.

"Heinrichs, Heinrichs, yeah, might be."

"It should be. My brother was Lothar Heinrichs. You do remember him, don't you? Or wasn't he important enough to remember?"

Lyle said nothing.

"Pick up that picture I dropped on the ground when you punched me. Go on, take a look."

Lyle picked up the photo and turned it over to see a man in aviation gear standing beside an airplane.

"Does that refresh your memory?" Erich asked.

"Let him up, Ed," Lyle said. "He's not a spy."

Ed released his hold, and Erich stood up, brushed himself off, picked up his hat and put it on.

"Who is he?"

"Lyle knows exactly who I am," Erich said. "In North Africa when he got that crew lost, my brother was one of the pilots who died. I swore I'd get revenge." He turned to Lyle and said, "I've kept track of you, and when I heard you were here in Brazil, I knew I'd have my chance."

"Well, here I am. What do you want to do, kill me?"

"No. Oh, I've thought about it for years, but I can't stoop to that level. I just wanted to make you face me, see what kind of a fella you are, see if you have any remorse."

"Don't you think I feel bad about that?" Lyle

asked. "It's haunted me for years, and I've been running ever since."

"That's what you're doing here in this part of town?"

"I suppose it is. At least somewhat."

Erich reached inside his jacket. Ed snapped to attention, ready to make a grab for his hand, but all he pulled out was a pack of cigarettes. He offered one to Lyle, then offered him a light. "I just recently learned of some new information about the accident. It may make you feel better. It helped me, helped me quit hating you. Do you know about the compass?"

"No."

"The officials went through the plane looking for any kind of malfunction that would've gotten it so far off course. It took a long while, but finally they discovered the compass was off by at least fifteen degrees."

"I swung the compass before the flight and it checked out fine, right on the money. What could've happened?"

"Nobody knows," Erich said. "The mechanic that checked over the plane before the flight was there when you checked the compass. He verified that. But something malfunctioned a few days later. Sabotage is one theory, another is the extreme heat in the desert. But something malfunctioned."

"I never heard that. I guess I tried to put the whole

deal out of my mind. I went over and over it in my mind and could never figure out what I did wrong. I was accused of being hungover. I wasn't. Sure, I got a habit, but it's been exaggerated. You know how people talk. I don't drink much the night before a flight. Ed knows that. Yeah, I hit it hard sometimes when we're not flying the next day."

"He seems to be on the level," Ed said. "He's been pretty drunk on this trip a few times, but I've noticed it's always when we're not flying the next day."

Ed turned to Lyle. "I had reservations about you, at first. In fact, I was downright angry the captain signed you on. I heard the stories and had no reason not to believe them. I figured you'd be drunk most of the time. I see I was wrong. You're drunk just part of the time."

Lyle asked Erich, "How'd you know to find me here?"

"I know your habits. I followed you here, and I saw someone else watching you fellas. A shadowy kind of person lurking about in the crowds. It was obvious he was watching your moves."

"Can you describe him?" Ed asked.

"Glasses, hair combed back, and a scar on his left cheek. Once, I saw another fella with him, dark hair, clean-shaven, tall, thin."

"Holtz!" Ed exclaimed. "And the other fella must

be Frederick."

"Who are they?" Erich asked.

"Nazis. They've been following us; we think they're with CSAA."

"CSAA?"

"Colombia and South American Airways," Lyle said. "They have a lot of German backing and want to expand deeper into South America. We think they're trying to sabotage us so they can take over."

"Nazis!" Erich exclaimed. "I've been begging my parents to move out of Germany since they've gotten into power. They're going to take over the country totally, and they'll persecute a lot of people. I can see it coming."

"What do you do for a living?" Ed asked.

"Import and export."

"Really? Say, maybe we can make some deals."

While Ed and Erich discussed business, Lyle found his way back to the hotel. He took his time, thinking about the events that had just transpired and about the faulty compass.

He allowed details that he'd tried to suppress for years to come back, and he found himself back in the desert, walking away from the crumpled plane lying in the forlorn sand. Out of fuel, the pilot, Lothar Heinrichs, and the copilot approached for a power-off landing, normally a routine situation. The hummock with a clump of weeds wasn't visible until the last instant, too late to avoid. The landing gear caught it and flipped the plane over. Stunned, Lyle crawled from the plane. He went back to help the pilots out, but it was too late. All he could do was take water canteens and head off for help. And he had walked away ever since.

~

The flight from Rio to Salvador and on to Fortaleza, where the crew spent the night, was uneventful, the engines running perfectly and the weather clear. All that changed in a hurry the next day, however, as they flew on after a quick stop in Sao Luis on their way to Belém.

Propaganda Radio

The radio blared with the leader's voice coming over the airwaves. People in stores and pubs paused in their activities, riveted with attention. People on sidewalks stopped and listened to the message as it fed through loudspeakers, and in homes, families gathered around radios at the prescribed time. The voice, rising and falling, a near whisper one moment, yelling the next, mesmerized all within hearing distance, the message stirring them to patriotism. End the dramatic unemployment, increase farm production, heal the economy. The suffering, they heard, was due to foreign entities who could not be trusted, reparations for the Great War, Jewish conspiracies, Communists, all people who must be feared. The fair-skinned citizens of the country must fight this enemy, fight at all costs and by whatever means needed to ensure the continuation of the chosen race.

The leader and his speeches were filmed, the newsreels shown in darkened theaters, printed verbatim in newspapers, his face on posters plastered across the nation. He and he alone would save Germany and proudly lead the country into its shining new future.

The broadcast ended. Radios returned to music. People resumed talking, quiet at first, contemplative, then gradually rising to normal tones, laughter here and there, a return to routine until the next broadcast.

Chapter Ten

Just after the city of João Pessoa passed below the port wing, Lyle called, "Plane, nine o'clock low. Looks like it might be our German friends."

Off and below the port wing, a single-engine plane flew nearly parallel and at the same pace as the S-42, gradually drifting in closer.

"It's the Germans," Captain Williams said.

"Wonder what they want now," Jack said. "Hey, looks like they're getting in kinda close."

The captain nodded. "Yeah. I can see the two men, see their faces through the canopy. The one on the right is sliding open his window."

"What?" Jack asked.

"Captain," Ed called, "better get ready for evasive action. They're gonna start shooting!"

The plane now flew just a few feet off the wing, slightly below, and the man in the right seat pointed a long-barreled pistol upward at the cockpit of the S-42.

"Full power!" Captain Williams yelled. "My airplane!"

Jack relinquished the controls, reached overhead, and slammed the throttle and propeller levers full forward as the captain hauled back on the control wheel. The plane nosed upward in a steep climb, temporarily evading the German plane and its gunman. But in a moment, the German plane drew alongside once again.

Ed tore off his headset and rushed to the rear of the plane, clinging to anything he could to steady himself, as Captain Williams put the plane through evasive maneuvers, climbing and diving and turning, bouncing Ed around like a pinball. He staggered his way past Lyle, who was desperately trying to keep charts and pencils on his table throughout the plane's gyrations. Finally at the rear of the plane, Ed found what he was looking for packed among the supplies and spare parts—a high-powered hunting rifle. He grabbed the rifle and a box of ammunition, and then made his way, bouncing side to side, back to the flight deck. He ordered Captain Williams out of the pilot's seat—the captain practically rolled out of the seat while Jack took the controls—and, in one swift motion, slid open the pilot's window, loaded the gun and aimed it at the German plane. The Germans, not yet aware of what Ed was doing, pulled in even closer, the gunman taking careful aim at the flight deck.

Through the evasive maneuvering, the S-42 was down to less than a thousand feet above the ground. The coastline of rocks, trees, and sand rushed by while the German machine nimbly maneuvered and then closed in so the gunman would have a good close-range shot. The Messerschmitt, now just ahead of the S-42's port wing, closed in to half a wingspan away, the tail of the plane dangerously close to the outboard propeller—so close that the eyes of the gunman were visible as well as the glint of sun off the barrel of his weapon.

"Hold it steady, Jack!" Ed yelled. "Steady!"

Before the German could get off his shot, Ed fired. The crack of the rifle echoed throughout the plane, followed by the smell of burned gunpowder. Harold jumped and if not for the seat belt would've come at least a foot out of the seat. Ed fired again, aiming for the Messerschmitt's engine, and got off three more quick shots. The bullets hit home. Smoke and oil poured from under the plane's cowl and blew back in the slipstream, leaving a black, smoky trail as the plane pulled away and went downward. All eyes except Harold's watched the German machine as it headed earthward toward the strip of sand along the coast. The plane touched down, gear up, in a spray of sand and water, and jerked to a stop. The canopy flew open. The two men jumped out and ran from the smoking machine.

Ed closed the window and said calmly, matter-of-factly, to the captain, "You can have your seat back." He then methodically unloaded the remaining bullets from the gun, placed them in the ammo box, and turned to head back to the rear compartment. Then he stopped and said, "I guess that makes me an ace. I shot down four planes in the war."

"What's going on?" Harold asked, panic in his voice.

"Butz shot down the German plane," Jack said.

"What?"

"He shot down the German plane. They were shooting at us; it was self-defense."

"Radio," Captain Williams said, "try to contact the navy ship and tell them what happened and get coordinates from Lyle. The navy will want to get the men, if possible."

"Yes sir."

Captain Williams then called to Lyle, "Make sure we're back on the correct course after all that maneuvering."

"You're headed the right general direction. Soon as I get things back in order here, I'll give you a precise heading."

Ed returned to the flight deck, took his seat among the valves, gauges, and dials, and resumed his scanning of the instruments and his plotting of the fuel flow as if nothing out of the ordinary had happened. The smell of gunpowder dissipated, taking with it the last remaining evidence of the dogfight fought with hand-held weapons.

The men remained quiet as they continued on to Belém. Finally Harold announced, "Got word from the navy ship. They weren't far away, so they got to the crash quickly. They found the plane but no one around, so they're going to leave ashore a group of men to track them."

"Thanks," the captain said. "And fellas, we all need to keep this to ourselves. I won't report this to Wilcox. We'll wait until we get back, and I'll report it directly to the old man."

The rest of the flight to Belém was uneventful. The coastline of Brazil passed by beneath the port wing, mile after mile and hour after hour until the city appeared in the distance. The afternoon cumulus buildup had been minimal with no rain showers to dodge, and the air remained relatively smooth—a perfect day for flying, interrupted only by the excitement of the German encounter.

Jack made a smooth landing in Belém. A couple

of US Navy sailors greeted them and informed them that they and two other navy men were on hand to guard the plane and assist with inspecting the load of coffee that would be taken aboard the following morning. The crew, overnight bags in hand, found a cab to take them to the hotel. While in the lobby checking in, the mayor, Rafael, and his assistant, Carlos, entered, sweating and appearing slightly out of breath.

"Greetings again," said the mayor. "We didn't expect to see you—uh, I mean, see you so soon."

"Really? Well, here we are. And we had a smooth flight," the captain replied.

"No problems?" Carlos inquired.

"No."

"Ah, well, that is good to hear." Rafael pulled out a white handkerchief and wiped sweat from his brow. "Would you and your men like to dine with us this evening?" he continued. "Compliments of the City of Belém."

"We would be glad to join you. What time?"

"Seven o'clock. The café is two blocks down. The building may not look like much, but the food, it is excellent."

"We'll be there."

The next morning, the navy guards helped inspect the burlap bags of coffee that were to go on board the plane. Most of the bags contained nothing but coffee beans, but half a dozen contained some illegal drugs, as well as cash, in American dollars, buried deep within the one hundred pounds of beans. The loading took most of the morning, each bag being opened, inspected, and reclosed. The navy men and the S-42 crew formed a fire-brigade style line and loaded the coffee aboard. They stacked the bags along the cabin walls, leaving an aisle down the middle, and secured them with netting.

After loading, Captain Williams ordered refueling. He and Ed inspected the fuel, making sure it was aviation gasoline, free of water and other contaminants—he was taking no chances. This port of call made him uneasy just as it had on the way down. And the mayor and his assistant were absent for the morning's activities, just as they'd been absent the night before. Though they'd not met the crew as promised, the meal had been paid for. A small price not to have to face the crew and squirm under questioning.

Next stop would be Maracaibo, where they'd refuel and spend the night before turning northward to Nassau.

~

About fifteen minutes into the flight from Maracaibo heading directly to Nassau, Lyle said, "We've got an oil leak on number three. Pretty bad. It's running back to the trailing edge in a steady stream."

"Roger," the captain responded. "Mechanic, go to the cabin and check it out."

"Roger, Captain." Ed made his way back to the cabin where Lyle pointed out the stream of oil.

Ed called back, "Captain, we've got to shut it down."

"Roger."

Ed hurried back to his station so he could shut off the fuel to the engine and secure it.

"We can't go on with that oil leak," the captain said. "We need to turn around and go back to Maracaibo."

"We're over maximum landing weight," Ed said.

"We'll dump fuel. Figure how much we need to get rid of."

The maximum landing weight of the S-42, as with many larger aircraft, was less than the maximum takeoff weight. Under normal conditions more than enough fuel would be burned off to reduce the weight before landing. By landing overweight, the plane could suffer structural damage upon contact with the water.

"Dump fuel?" asked Ed.

"Affirmative."

Ed hesitated, then said, "Navigator."

"Go ahead."

"Keep an eye on the dumped fuel. Make sure it flows away and clear of the wing."

"Roger. Will do."

Ed opened the dump valves and fuel flowed from the tanks and out into the slipstream. "Navigator, how's it look?" he asked.

"So far nothing unusual. I can see the fuel coming out."

"Keep an eye on it." Ed fidgeted in his seat and his hands rested on the dump valves.

"Mechanic," the captain called. "Are you expecting a problem?"

"Not necessarily, but we need to keep an eye on it."

A few minutes went by while the fuel streamed out of the plane and flowed away into the air in a fine mist.

"Shut it down!" Lyle yelled. "Shut off the dump!"

Ed's hands flew as he closed the valves. Once shut, he asked, "Lyle, what's going on?"

"The fuel started to build up at the rear of the wing, and I swear I could see it getting sucked in. Now it's dripping into the cabin! It's dripping from under the wing."

"Shut down the electrics!" Ed yelled. "Captain, the electrics master! Off!"

"Roger," Captain Williams said. "Electrics off."

Harold's radios went dead. "What now?" he asked.

The inside of the plane began to reek of highly volatile aviation gasoline.

"All we can do is wait," Ed said. "Wait for the fuel to clear out. I'll go to the back and crack open the cabin hatch, get some air moving and get the fumes out."

The pilots threw open the sliding windows on the flight deck. Ed hurried to the rear of the plane, unlatched the entry hatch atop the fuselage, and propped it open a few inches. Air began to move to the rear, carrying the gasoline fumes with it. The men didn't talk. All they could do was wait and hope an explosion wouldn't happen. The stench of fuel gradually faded from the inside of the plane, and as the smell faded, hope increased that the plane and the men wouldn't be obliterated in a fireball.

The captain broke the silence. "I guess we'll circle to burn off fuel." He had to speak loudly to be heard since the intercom was dead due to the electricity being shut down.

Lyle poked his head in through the flight deck door. "The coffee's getting wet."

"I've got a tarp stashed," Ed said. "We can cover the coffee with it."

"Good thing we don't have passengers on board," Jack said. "They'd get a gasoline bath."

"Sikorsky is going to have to make a modification," the captain said. "Ed was right, the dump system is dangerously flawed. Pacific Airways got an S-42 just after we did, so we need to alert them to the problem. I'll get on the horn to Nassau as soon as we land."

The plane droned on in lazy circles, around and around in order to burn off enough weight in fuel. The inside of the plane still smelled of gasoline. Though the cabin began to clear of the explosive fumes, there was no way of knowing what was happening inside the wing. The men didn't know if there were pools of fuel trapped inside, if the vapors would reach the hot engines, or if the wing was airing out, the danger of explosion lessening. All they could do was circle and wait.

After droning around and around for an hour and a half, Jack manually lowered the flaps, brought the big machine in for an uneventful landing on three engines, and taxied up to the dock where the plane was secured. Captain Williams went into the harbor office to make a call to Nassau to apprise them of the situation while Ed, with assistance from the other men, began troubleshooting the problem.

After reaching and probing around inside the engine nacelle, Ed proclaimed to the three others standing atop the wing, "Aha! Here it is; I found the culprit!"

"What is it, Butz?" Jack asked.

"Broken oil line. See?" Ed pointed to a split in a metal line that went from the oil tank to the engine. "Must have been a weak spot, and engine vibration caused it to split. No way to detect it until it broke. First time I had this happen, a plane aborting a flight. At least we weren't on a scheduled run."

"Do you have a spare?" Harold asked.

"As a matter of fact, I do."

"We will help you fix the plane, *señor*," a man called up to Ed as he walked along the top of the fuselage toward the trailing edge of the wing, a new oil line in hand. A group of four or five men milled about on the dock, peering upward with eager eyes to try to get a glimpse of the goings-on. They chatted and pointed and scratched their heads and were eager to give assistance, assistance that would give the men prestige and bragging rights by helping to repair the big silver machine. "If there's anything you need, *señor*, we will get it."

"*Gracias*," Ed said. "I think we have what we need. But if not, we'll let you know."

Ed climbed up on the wing, hesitated, and then,

turning to the men, said, "*Amigos*, could you find something that will clean oil off the engine? We've got a big mess inside the cowl."

"*Si*, we will do that." The group of men scurried off to find solvent, rags, and towels.

Ed walked across the wing to number three engine. "That will keep them busy for a while."

Captain Williams had returned and joined the rest of the crew on top of the wing. "They're really wanting to help, aren't they?"

"Yeah. I knew they were itching to climb up here, but I don't want them running around all over the wing."

"You really need solvent?"

"Not really, but it wouldn't be a bad idea to clean away some of this oil. Make it easier to find a leak."

By the time Ed had a new oil line installed, the group of men reappeared with a can of solvent and a pile of rags of various colors and materials. There may have been some wives about town suddenly missing scarves and handkerchiefs. Ed climbed down from the wing onto the fuselage and then onto the dock where he thanked the men profusely, gathered up the can of solvent and the pile of rags, and made his way back atop the wing. The group of men, now satisfied that they got to help heal the sick bird, wandered off into the distance.

After Ed had finished the repairs and he and Harold had wiped the oil from inside the cowl, it was time for a test run. Jack took the copilot's seat and looked back over his shoulder to catch Ed's signals. Captain Williams manned the mechanic's station for engine start, while Ed and Harold went back atop the wing. Ed gave the pilots the signal; the engine cranked over and fired up immediately. With Harold helping to secure him, Ed peered into the engine compartment, reaching in to feel the line for the oil moisture. He gave the signal to increase engine speed, and the blast from the propeller blew his hair and flapped his coverall's collar while he peered and probed, searching for telltale signs of leaking oil.

He signaled to cut the engine, and the propeller jerked to a stop. The hurricane-force wind died down, and Ed signaled all was well. With Harold's assistance, he buttoned up the engine cowl, then clambered, toolbox in hand, back into the airplane and to the flight deck, Harold right behind him.

"It looks good," Ed said. "Get this thing refueled, and we're all set."

"We'll get fuel so we'll be set for morning," Captain Williams said. "It's too late to start out now."

After refueling, the men caught a ride to the hotel where Lyle had gone much earlier to reserve rooms. Once there, they headed to their rooms and threw their bags on the beds, then congregated in the lobby to go eat. All except Lyle, who was nowhere to be found.

"Where do you suppose he is?" Jack asked.

"Bet you have a good idea," Harold said.

"Yeah. Booze or women."

"Or both."

"As long as he's back by morning. That's all that's important," Ed said.

"And sober," Jack added.

Ed excused himself directly after the meal and wandered off into the dark corners of the city on some unannounced mission to make new contacts, connect with old contacts, make deals, and procure items of which other men could only dream.

The men, except for Ed Butz, never saw Lyle the rest of the evening. The last they saw of him, he was walking up the dock to catch a ride to the hotel, overnight bag and flight kit in hand, jacket slung over a shoulder, smoke from his Camel trailing behind. The men, except Ed, and Lyle, who seemed to have vanished, didn't venture out far during the evening. After supper, they strolled through the nearby streets, peering in shop windows and watching street performers. They returned to the hotel after grabbing a sweet dessert at a bakery.

Captain Williams knocked on the door to Jack's

room.

"Come in."

"Jack," the captain said, "You know I've been giving things a lot of thought recently."

"I know you have."

"I'm resigning as chief pilot. I'll turn in my resignation tomorrow. I want to fly the line, be on a regular schedule. Jack, I'm promoting you to captain and recommending you for the job of chief pilot. That is, if you want it."

"Well, I'm honored," Jack said. "But I've never thought about it. Being chief, I suppose I'd be making all the survey flights. I don't know. There's a lot of paperwork to the job, a lot of responsibility. I figured I'd be making the Havana flight for a long time to come."

"It'd be a pay rise. And you won't get bored."

"I know."

"Think it over."

"I will."

"Oh, and the promotion to captain is in effect immediately."

"Thank you, sir."

The next morning at daybreak, the men went to the plane to go through the preflight checks for their second attempt to leave Maracaibo, all except Lyle Ellison, who'd simply vanished. He'd walked off into the tropical night and blended into the crowds. The captain checked his room that morning. Empty. Bed unused. Gear and travel bag gone.

~

The men lingered for a few moments on the dock. Harold packed fresh tobacco in his pipe.

"Wonder what happened to Ellison," he said as he worked to get the tobacco just right.

"I ran into him last night," Ed said. "He was headed to the dockyard. Said a freighter captain paid him in cash to take over for the ship's injured navigator. That's the story he gave me, anyway. You do remember he's actually a maritime navigator."

"That cash in hand must've been a temptation," Jack said.

"No doubt it was a big influence." Ed clamped down on a fresh cigar, lit it and tossed the spent match into the water.

"I thought he'd go to Pacific Airways." Harold stuck his pipe into the corner of his mouth and lit it with his Zippo.

"What I'd heard too," Captain Williams said. He shrugged and added, "But who knows." He scanned the early morning sky, then announced, "Let's go, fellas." The men gathered up overnight bags and flight gear and boarded the plane.

After takeoff and making a pass over the town and the crowd of spectators at the dock, the plane turned northward toward Nassau and home.

By the time the men reached the eastern tip of Cuba, the cumulus were building up ahead of them, towering and roiling into the upper reaches of the atmosphere, much too high for the plane to fly over. Spaces between the clouds filled in quickly, blocking any means of passage, and the crew wasn't going to intentionally fly through them. The only way to continue to Nassau was to divert around the towering clouds. The men were so close to home—only about two and a half hours to go and they would touch down in the blue waters of Nassau. But the impending storm threatened to delay them, putting off their return to familiar surroundings. The sky ahead grew dark, almost black, punctuated by brilliant, blinding flashes of lightning—a place they didn't want to be.

After receiving a report of clearing skies over Havana, the men changed course. Jack, who'd been navigating from his copilot's seat, the chart spread out in front of him, determined the new course. Harold manned the navigation radio. Between the two, they were getting along without Lyle, though it placed more demand on each of them.

Captain Williams banked the plane over to the

new heading, the storm clouds now to their starboard, and a faint glimpse of sunlight peeked out ahead.

~

"Nassau radio. Survey flight twenty miles south inbound for landing. Over," Jack called.

"Survey flight, go ahead. Over," welcomed a woman's voice with a Jamaican accent.

"Nassau radio. It's so good to hear your voice, Vivian. Would you give us a weather report, please? Over."

"Survey flight, welcome home! Scattered cumulus. Wind two-six-zero at eight. Out."

"Sure feels good to hear Vivian and know we're almost home," Jack said.

Captain Williams agreed. "It sure does."

The sun was low in the sky, the final leg of the trip having taken longer than anticipated due to the storm. Though they'd hoped to get around the back side of the storm within a short distance, the men had to fly all the way to Havana and take on fuel. Now, in the softening light of the lowering sun, only a few puffy cumulus dotted the sky, and they were dissipating quickly, the perfect setting for the end of an odyssey. Soon Nassau appeared over the nose of the aircraft, beckoning, welcoming, calling the men home. One more landing. One more time to ease the plane down on a perfect glide path, and then touch down in a spray of water, slow, and ease gently to the dock.

"Captain Smith, you want to bring it in?" Captain Williams asked.

"Sure. But you should have the honor."

"No, I don't need to. It's your airplane." With that command, Jack set aside the navigation chart, took the controls, and guided the plane toward final approach. He eased back the throttles, set the propellers, and pitched the plane to attain the proper approach speed, then called for the first notch of flaps. He took quick glances at the gauges and focused intently out over the nose of the plane, looking to maintain the correct sight picture for approach, while he made small adjustments with the control wheel and throttles—adjustments so small as to be nearly imperceptible. He'd learned well from Captain Williams.

After securing the plane, the four men exited the aircraft and made their way up the ramp toward the terminal. Now back at home base, the trek behind them, they began to relax. Fatigue lined their faces and showed in their walk, the men worn down after days in the air and nights in unfamiliar surroundings.

"Look at the restaurant!" Jack exclaimed. "They're

busy."

Nearly every table was full. Patrons dressed in fine clothes ate at tables with linen tablecloths, china plates, and real silverware, while waiters in white jackets scurried about, taking orders, serving food, and pouring coffee. People who'd arrived on late-afternoon flights, as well as locals who enjoyed the first-class amenities, filled the place.

When the four men, flight gear in hand, reached the top of the stairs to the Caribbean Airways offices, a chorus of "Welcome home!" came from the small group of people gathered to meet them. In addition to Vivian and Gail, Don Wilcox, Roger Brown, and several of the pilots who'd hung around after their flights waited for them. And Jennifer was there.

Captain Williams dropped his flight gear to grab ahold of her as she ran to his arms. He picked her up, spun around, and set her back down. Then they hugged each other tightly.

Ed drew Wilcox and Roger Brown aside, explaining to them the urgency in contacting Pacific Airways to follow up on the information Captain Williams had already conveyed about the hazards of dumping fuel on the S-42.

"You don't know?" Roger asked.

"Know what?"

"The Pacific Airways plane exploded this

morning. They had a similar situation as yours, an oil leak on one engine and they were dumping fuel to land. They'd radioed their base saying that was what they were doing."

Ed frowned. "Any survivors?"

"No. But only the flight crew was onboard."

Ed sighed and shook his head. "The plane has to go back to New Jersey to Sikorsky for modifications. We can't fly passengers until the problem is fixed."

"We've been in contact with Sikorsky and they assured me they have a fix," Roger said. "They've tested it, but Ed, you need to go and make sure it's right."

"We'll go to New York in a couple of days," Captain Williams said. "Tomorrow we'll make a quick run to Miami. Have a load of coffee that needs to come off."

"Supposed to have some new crews coming in within a week," Roger said. "Radio operators and flight mechanics, as well as pilots. You and Ed and Harold will be busy training all those new fellas."

"Well, somebody will," Captain Williams said. Roger gave him a puzzled look, but the captain said nothing about resigning as chief pilot.

"Captain Williams," Wilcox said, "the old man wants you to check in with him."

"Now?"

"He said as soon as you got back. Use the phone in my office."

The captain shut the door behind him and called the New York City office. John Trapp answered.

"Mister Trapp, Max Williams."

"Yes, Captain. How was the flight home?"

"Had to divert around some weather, but otherwise very good."

"Williams, the main reason I want to talk to you is about the incident with the German plane that I heard about from military sources. You and your crew keep that to yourselves. The navy did catch the two spies and are holding them. From what we can understand, Germany will keep quiet about the incident. They don't want the publicity and don't want to have to admit they're trying to get a hold in the Western Hemisphere. And our government doesn't want to admit to us shooting down a foreign plane, even though it was self-defense."

"Understood, sir. I've already sworn my men to secrecy."

"Good. I think if we cooperate, we can maintain peace."

"I hope you're right, sir."

"Good evening, Captain."

"Good evening, sir."

While the captain was on the phone, a couple

of the pilots introduced themselves to Harold. On finding out he was going to be in charge of communications and radio equipment, they asked questions about the new radios they'd heard about. Harold answered their questions, tentatively at first, but the more he talked about radio waves and signals, the more animated he became, and soon he had the pipe out of his mouth and on an ashtray on the table in a corner of the room. He put to use a pad of paper and a pencil on the table and began drawing diagrams and writing math formulas as he talked. The pilots listened intently, looking at the diagrams and asking more questions, which Harold answered excitedly.

Gail gave Jack a quick hug. Then she stepped back to stand beside a pilot, a new pilot Jack didn't know. "Jack," Gail said, "this is Sam Monroe. Sam, this is Jack Smith. He's been with Caribbean Air for a while now, and he was just promoted to captain."

Sam extended his hand. "Good to meet you, Captain Smith."

"Good to meet you too." The men shook hands. "You're new here."

"Yes. Training on the Freeport flight."

"I started there too. That's the run most of us begin on. It was nice being home every night."

"I'm single, so it don't make no difference if I'm home every day or not. Course, I'm seein' Miss

Rogers," he said, turning to Gail.

"Oh?"

"Yeah. I met her the first day I was here. You know, Wilcox showed us around and introduced us to people. That's when I met her."

"When was that? When did you start?"

"Five days ago. Yeah, been here five days now."

"Gail's a great woman."

"She is."

Jack turned his attention to movement in the doorway. A familiar figure appeared, and he looked again to make sure he wasn't imagining things. "Sally?" he exclaimed.

Sally Wong stood in the doorway. She looked different, and Jack realized she wasn't wearing her waitressing attire but a long print dress, and she had her hair down, the black hair cascading down nearly to her waist. She looked even prettier than usual.

Jack took her into the hallway, where they'd have a bit of privacy. "Sally, what are you doing here? How'd you know we'd be back today?"

"I called here a few days ago and talked to someone, a woman named Gail, and she told me when you were due in. I've been here a couple of days waiting since you got delayed by mechanical trouble."

"You talked with Gail, huh?"

"Yes. She seems like a nice woman and was very

helpful."

"How'd you get here?"

"By boat. I can't afford a ticket for a flight, but the boat trip was fine. Jack, I just had to get here and see you as soon as you got back. I'm so sorry. I made a mistake, and I hope you will forgive me."

"Mistake? What do you mean? Forgive you for what?"

"When I told you we couldn't see each other, that we could only be friends. I haven't been able to stop thinking about you since that evening, and if you'll forgive me, and if you still want to, I'd like to see you. You know, have a date with you."

"But what about your marriage this summer?"

"I called that off. It's something I should've done a long time ago, but I was too afraid until I met you. You helped me realize I was doing what was expected, not what was right. Jack, do you still want to see me?"

"You bet I do!"

"Oh, I'm so relieved. I was afraid you'd want nothing to do with me after the way I treated you."

"You treated me fine, Sally. You did what you had to do at the time, and I fully understand."

"Thank you, Jack."

"So how have your folks taken the news?"

"They were pretty upset at first, but after a bit they saw how happy and relieved I was, so they kind of came around."

"Did you tell them you're going to be seeing me?"

"Yes, I did. Well, I told them I wanted to see you if you were still interested."

"And how did they take that news?"

"Because they know you and like you, they took it pretty well. I'm not going to lie, they were disappointed at first that I wasn't going to be seeing a Chinese fella, but they're beginning to get used to the idea. Jack, don't be afraid to see my folks. They'll treat you as nice as they always have. Father is looking forward to you and Captain Williams coming into the restaurant again. He says you two are the nicest pilots he knows."

"I'll bet we're the only pilots he knows."

"Jack, that's funny."

"How's your brother, Walter?"

"Oh, he's doing very well. He told me to tell you he wants a plane ride too."

"I'll be glad to take him up."

"Sally, come on in with me and meet the crew." He took her by the hand and led her into the communications room. Gradually the room went silent, one by one, as each person shifted attention to Jack and this unknown woman with him.

"Everyone, I'd like you to meet Sally Wong."

After the meeting and greeting, Captain Jack

Smith excused himself and walked down the hallway, a subtle though confident swagger about him. He walked on down the stairs and through the terminal out into the warm evening air, the sun almost touching the western horizon, Sally Wong at his side. A row of S-38s rocked gently at their docks, resting for the following day's flights, and at the far end, at the new big dock, the S-42 quietly awaited its next adventure.

A Note from the Author

Did you enjoy my book?

If so, I would be very grateful if you could write a review and publish it at your point of purchase. Your review, even a brief one, will help other readers to decide whether or not they'll enjoy my work. Large numbers of reviews are vital for helping indie books find readers, so I appreciate every little one and thank you for your time.

Would you like a free ebook and notifications of new releases from my publisher, AIA Publishing?

If so, please visit www.aiapublishing.com and click the button to subscribe to notifications of new publications. You'll receive a free ebook of *Worlds Within Worlds* by Tahlia Newland. Of course, your information will never be shared, and the publisher won't inundate you with emails, just let you know of new releases.

www.ingramcontent.com/pod-product-compliance
Lightning Source LLC
Chambersburg PA
CBHW030803200726
48285CB00014B/539